GN00792160

ALWENA'S GARDEN

Mary Oldham

PONT BOOKS

First Impression—1997

ISBN 1 85902 438 6

© Mary Oldham

Mary Oldham has asserted her right under the Copyright, Designs and Patents Act, 1988, to be identified as Author of this Work.

This book is published with the support of the Arts Council of Wales.

Printed in Wales at
Gomer Press, Llandysul, Ceredigion

For my sister Angela Wilkins,
and Derek, Rosemary, Louisa and Stuart
A Cardiganshire Family

Chapter One

'Fortunately the prognosis,' said the doctor, folding up his stethoscope, 'is good.'

He addressed Alwena Morgan's parents, who were sitting on either side of her like a committee.

He never speaks to *me*, thought Alwena. He never tells *me* that the prognosis is good. She stared coldly at the doctor. For the past two years people had been standing over her and telling each other that the prognosis was bad, or good, or better than expected. I'm a girl, not a prognosis, she thought.

It was very tiring, being stuck with this prognosis, like an unwanted pet you couldn't find a home for. Alwena saw it as a kind of octopus, which lurked grumbling in its corner most of the time, but which every now and then would surge and swell into life, wrapping its scaly tentacles around her and squeezing until the air drained from her lungs and her joints went limp.

'I hope you're doing your exercises regularly,' said the doctor, speaking hastily as though he had noticed her accusing look. 'We need to build up those muscles.'

'Oh, she is,' replied her father. 'She's very good about it. And we take her swimming, of course. We don't let her overdo it, mind.'

Alwena scowled. She hated swimming. She hated having to wear a swimsuit, which revealed her matchstick legs and tennis ball knees. She hated having to feel thankful because she was the least handicapped of all the children who used the pool on Special Club night. She hated the way her father always insisted on swimming up and down beside her in case she got cramp.

'I don't think they have the water warm enough at the Sports Centre,' said Alwena's mother.

'The weather has helped, I daresay, being so hot all summer,' said the doctor. 'You're walking very well indeed, Alwena, that's very good. Now then, what about the old morning stiffness? Are you finding the tablets a help?'

'Yes, thank you,' replied Alwena quickly, before her father could report on this also. She closed her hands around each other, gently touching the swollen knuckles. They felt tender again today, but not too painful.

'She's very good about taking them. I'm sure it's a help,' said her father.

'She needs to eat well. Plenty of cheese and fruit—'

She, thought Alwena. It's always *She*. Next time I'm going to make them let me see him on my own. I'm old enough.

'But what about the future, Doctor?' demanded Mrs Morgan. 'What about when she gets older? Will she grow out of it?' She ignored her husband's not-in-front-of-Alwena frown. 'Will she grow up—you know, *develop* properly?'

'There's no reason why Alwena shouldn't grow up in a perfectly natural way,' said the doctor. Alwena noticed him avoiding the word 'normal'. 'As I say, the prognosis for this sort of juvenile arthritis is quite good. There may be the occasional relapse, but the thing to do is for Alwena to get back to leading an ordinary life like other children—other girls of her age.'

8

'Would it help,' Mrs Morgan interrupted again, 'if we moved to a warmer climate?'

Her husband said at once, 'I don't know how we could live anywhere healthier than we do. Pure mountain air, no pollution.'

'And rain and fog from October to May.'

'I believe the important thing,' said the doctor diplomatically, 'is for Alwena to get back to normal as soon as she can. She's missed nearly two years of school, for one thing. All her friends will be leaving her behind.'

'I won't get left behind,' said Alwena. 'I do a lot of reading.'

'Her mother's been doing lessons with her,' said her father. 'The computer's been a great help. She's very bright, you know.'

'It will be easier if she transfers to Abercoed,' said her mother. 'The school building is all on one level, for one thing, not like Aberystwyth. It'll be much easier for her to get about.'

'I'm not at all happy about that,' said her father at once. 'You know we thought it would be best if she carried on at Aber after we moved.'

'But that was before her illness. We've got to look at other factors now—the travelling, for instance.'

Alwena's father's face went tight with annoyance. He hated being argued with.

'I don't know what you've got against Ysgol Abercoed,' pursued her mother. 'You went there yourself! And T. J. Mostyn teaches there! You can't say it isn't a good school.'

'Hm! I've got my own opinions about that!'

'I don't mind doing lessons at home,' said Alwena. 'T. J. Mostyn comes to our house all the time helping in the library. He tells me a lot of history. I did a project on the lead mines at Maesderwen.'

She did not know what would be worse, going back to school in Aberystwyth and being stared at by people who knew her, or going to a new school and being stared at by people who did not.

'It's not just lessons, is it, doctor?' said her mother. 'She needs to be back among her own age group. She'll be fifteen in the spring. She's been on her own too long. It's not as if she lives just round the corner and her friends can drop in any time.'

Alwena's father was shaking his head angrily. 'That's not the point,' he said. 'Look how ill she's been. She's not ready for the rough-and-tumble of school yet, let alone a new school altogether. You said it was important she doesn't overdo it, didn't you, doctor?'

'We'll talk to the school about it,' said Mrs Morgan. 'Both schools, if you like. They must have facilities for this sort of thing.'

'That's the best thing,' agreed the doctor. 'It probably wouldn't be a good idea until after Christmas, anyway,' he added quickly, before Mr Morgan could speak again. 'Now, let's see, when's your next appointment at the orthopaedic hospital, December? Shall we see how things are after that?'

Saved, thought Alwena. There were times when she was still happy to let her father look after things for her. She smiled at him and his face began to relax.

'And how are things coming along at Plas Idaleg?' asked the doctor as they all stood up and Mr Morgan helped Alwena on with the fat duck-down ski jacket he had given her as an early Christmas present. 'How's the fund-raising going?'

All traces of irritation vanished from Mr Morgan's face. 'We're about to send off the National Lottery application,' he said eagerly.

'Come on, Roscoe, the doctor's got other people to see,' said Mrs Morgan. 'Don't start him off,' she told the doctor.

'Come and see for yourself, any time,' said Mr Morgan. 'We're snowed under with books people have donated for the library at the moment. A lot of it's rubbish, of course, but you'd be surprised—'

'Roscoe!'

Ten minutes later they were in the car in the long queue of Friday afternoon traffic pulling up the hill out of Aberystwyth. Mr Morgan turned the heater and the demister full on as the rain lashed down. 'Are you keeping warm, *cariad*?' he asked Alwena.

'Yes, thank you,' she replied. 'My new jacket's lovely and cosy.'

'Have you got that blanket well tucked in over your legs?'

'Yes, Dad.'

'What she needs,' said her mother, 'is more hot sunshine, never mind anoraks and blankets.'

'I'm fine, Mam,' said Alwena. 'I'm lovely and warm.'

'It's too damp where we are,' pursued her mother. 'Besides,' she added, giving her husband a meaningful look, 'it's not as if it hasn't happened before. In the past.'

There was a particular tone of voice that Alwena's parents used when they wanted to drop hints to each other over her head, which always put her on the alert.

'No, no, you've got it all wrong,' said Mr Morgan. 'It was when they took her away she got so much worse.' He frowned quickly at his wife. 'Anyway, times have changed. They didn't have proper medicine and orthopaedic hospitals in those days.'

'Hm,' said Mrs Morgan. Silence fell. In the back seat, Alwena memorised these two last remarks carefully. *It's not as if it hasn't happened before. It was when they took her away that she got so much worse.* They were talking about The Child again. She was not supposed to know about The Child.

'The rain's letting up,' said Mr Morgan presently, as they climbed into the hills, driving through small roadside hamlets named after chapels, Bethel and Seion and Moriah. 'Soon be home,' he said.

The road rose and dipped and twisted over the high moorland, the wind gusting across the car. Mr Morgan clung to the steering wheel. You don't drive a car in these hills, Alwena's brother David was fond of saying. You sail it.

Then quite suddenly they were in the shelter of the forest, a dark ocean of Sitka spruce splashed at the verges with the golden autumn rain of birch and hazel trees. The road became a tunnel with a high stone wall on one side and a Forestry Commission plantation on the other.

'T. J. isn't home yet,' said Alwena's father as they drove past the single-storey stone lodge with pointed windows which stood at the western entrance to the Plas Idaleg estate. The lodge was the home of T. J. Mostyn, the history teacher at Ysgol Abercoed. Alwena's mother often said she would swap houses with him any time, and only pretended to be joking, Alwena thought, because she knew how such remarks upset her husband.

Roscoe Morgan thought he lived in Paradise. Indeed, there were many who agreed with him. People who didn't spot the Italian connection often thought Plas Idaleg was called Plas Idyllic. 'How appropriate,' they would breathe, gazing at the huge, disintegrating Gothic mansion with its surroundings of mountain, forest and river. 'How Sublime, how Romantic, how Picturesque!' Somehow you knew the words had capital letters.

Alwena hated strangers saying how divine the house was and how lucky the Morgans were to live in it. She wanted to keep it a secret, a secret shared only by her family and T. J. Mostyn. Plas Idaleg was a magic house. They all felt it, even her mother for all she moaned about the cold and the damp and the inconvenience. When they were away from it they could never quite believe it existed, or that it would still be there on their return. Now, as the car rocked slowly along the potholed drive which wound down through the woods, and clanked over the cattle grid into the open parkland, they fell silent as they always seemed to in those few moments before the house appeared, in case one day it might not.

But there it was, quite solid and real in its ruined vastness, the marble and stone mansion with its colonnades and its battlemented roof, and the delicately carved stone arch which rose like a tiara over the great front doors. The rain had stopped and a slight mist was forming over the trees, shifting round the tall Italian bell tower which had been added on to the house in the nineteenth century and which had given Plas Idaleg its modern name.

'Imagine, if we get the Lottery money,' said Mr Morgan. 'The Italian wing completed at last. The whole house ablaze with lights. People working in the library. International symposia.'

'Central heating,' said Mrs Morgan.

I hope we don't get it, thought Alwena.

What would happen if they didn't? Plas Idaleg belonged to the University, a legacy it had not known quite what to do with apart from billeting the Morgans there to look after it. Then the possibility had come along of applying to the National Lottery for funds to turn it into what the prospectus called an International Study Centre for the Architectural Heritage of Wales.

Alwena hated the idea of hundreds of strangers swarming all over Plas Idaleg. The friends her brother David brought home in his vacations from University in Cardiff were bad enough, playing deafening music from morning to night and talking and laughing and leaving empty beer cans and half-eaten pizzas everywhere.

'It won't be like that,' her father would say. 'It will be a very serious, scholarly place. People will come for the peace and quiet.'

'You reckon!' David would say, roaring with laughter.

This always made her father furious and she didn't blame him.

The Morgans lived in a number of rooms which had once been known as the Steward's Quarters, situated at the back of the house overlooking a cobbled courtyard which you approached through a tumbledown brick archway.

'Oh look,' said Alwena as the car drove under the archway. 'Bedwyr's come home.'

Bedwyr was her donkey, who had the run of the estate and was sometimes not seen for several days, although the hay left out for him in one of the open barns always disappeared. At the sight of the car Bedwyr opened his mouth and brayed loudly. Inside the house, Olwen the bull terrier began to bark.

'Home at last,' said Mr Morgan. 'Stay there, Alwena, and I'll get your wheelchair. You're worn out.'

'No, I'm all right, I can walk all right. I'm a bit stiff from sitting in the car, that's all.'

'Let me carry you, then.'

'No! I can manage!'

But by the time she had reached the kitchen her strength had ebbed away. She barely made it to the chair by the kitchen range, and her father had to shout at poor Olwen for trying to climb on her lap to welcome her home. Her mother gave her a tablet with some hot milk, and nothing more was said that day about her going back to school.

*   *   *

Alwena awoke the following morning with a fuzzy head, not quite able to remember whether she had slept all night or not. That was the problem with having to take

15

tablets all the time, you never felt quite properly awake or asleep; you remembered bits of dreams and you could not tell whether they were memories of dreams or things that had really happened. Worse, there were times when your sleep obliterated all memory of your long illness; you awoke feeling deliciously cosy, but wide awake and looking forward to leaping out of bed and running out into the morning.

But then, with one painful twitch of an arm or leg, you remembered. You remembered the weeks of fever, the weeks of agony when you could hardly move at all, when your ankles, knees and wrists swelled and burned with pain and you could not bear anyone to touch you. You remembered the crutches, the wheelchair, the doctors and surgeons. The months in the orthopaedic hospital with your limbs being pulled and pushed and massaged by physiotherapists. The long, painful struggle to walk again.

Alwena moved her ankles carefully. The local physiotherapist, an exhaustingly cheerful woman called Pam who played hockey, had taught her a number of movements to do before getting out of bed, to loosen up her joints. After that there was a special way of rolling over to the edge of the bed, swinging her legs to the floor, then sitting up and taking several deep breaths to stop her getting congestion of the lungs.

She sat there for a few moments, looking round the bedroom in which she had spent most of the last two years of her life, apart from when she had been in hospital. Pinned on the wall, out of reach of the sun to stop them fading, were the rosettes she had won at riding school gymkhanas before her illness. There was a framed photograph, taken by her mother, of Alwena aged ten, mounted on a chestnut pony with a flying mane, clearing a fence in a jumping competition.

The picture was supposed to give her hope, to encourage her to get better so that she could ride again, but Alwena hardly noticed it these days. It might as well have been another person, another life.

Slippers. Dressing gown. One good thing, she was allowed to get up on her own now. She no longer had to endure her father lifting her out of bed and carrying her to the bathroom for her morning bath. A shower had been installed, with a seat and grip handles and an alarm buzzer, so that she could manage on her own on all but very bad days.

Her father was finding this harder to get used to than she was, which was why she listened carefully for the sound of his voice in the kitchen before before crossing the landing to the bathroom. Nonetheless, no sooner had she locked the door and turned on the shower than he came running upstairs.

'Are you sure you can manage?'

'Yes, Dad, I'm fine.'

'Don't forget to press the buzzer if you want any help.'

'I'm all *right*!'

'Well, be careful.' There was a pause. Alwena pressed her mouth shut and went on sitting under the warm water, turning a little to let it run down her back. After a moment she heard him go downstairs again. At least he had not tried the door. She was not supposed to lock the bathroom door, in case of accidents, but the idea of leaving it unlocked for anyone to walk in when they felt like it outraged her.

Alwena wondered if the Child's father had been like hers, incapable of leaving her alone.

The Child would have had a maid, if she lived here in the olden days, thought Alwena as she went downstairs. She wouldn't have needed her father to carry her about. Whoever she was, and whatever was wrong with her.

Because there must have been something, or why did Alwena's parents, or T. J. Mostyn come to that, never mention her except in little whispered remarks to each other when they thought Alwena was not listening?

'Hullo,' said Mrs Morgan to Alwena as she walked into the kitchen. 'I heard you in the shower. Good day?'

'Good, I think.' Alwena's illness had good days and bad days, which were unpredictable.

'Mind you take it easy today,' said her father. 'You got over-tired yesterday.' He smiled at her as he buttered a slice of toast, then went back to opening his mail. Alwena relaxed as she watched his attention shift from her to the day's work. 'T. J. will be here any minute,' he said. 'I'm hoping we can spend the whole day in the library. We must make a start on those books from the Roderick family.'

The library was one of the most famous rooms in the Plas. On account of the books, it was now the only room apart from the Morgans' quarters to be adequately heated. Alwena did her lessons with her mother there during the week.

Alwena liked the library, and she liked T. J. Mostyn.

Her father was never so fussy about things when T. J. was there. 'Can I come and help?' she asked.

'Better go out for a bit first,' said her mother. 'Get some fresh air. The fog's lifted. I'll take you out for a little ride on Bedwyr, if you like.'

Her mother and Pam the physiotherapist were both convinced that Alwena was longing to ride again and that the best medicine for her would be to have her own pony. Alwena's father said that a pony would be far too dangerous, they were unpredictable, self-willed creatures which would be sure to bolt or buck Alwena off. So they had compromised with Bedwyr the donkey.

Sitting on Bedwyr's back with her mother holding a leading rein was not what Alwena called riding. It made her feel like a five-year-old having a donkey ride on Borth beach. Bedwyr himself made it quite clear that he regarded being ridden as beneath him. However he was agreeable company so long as there was no saddle in sight and Alwena had grown very fond of him. He would follow her everywhere; he listened to everything she said and never minded her leaning on him when she got tired.

'I won't ride today. I'll just go for a walk down to the Parson's Bridge,' said Alwena.

'Well, wrap up warm. It may be sunny, but the wind's cold. And take your stick.'

Half an hour later Alwena walked out of the kitchen door and across the yard to the drive which led round to the front of the Plas where Bedwyr was grazing. This time last year she had still been spending most of her time in bed. She had almost forgotten what out-of-doors was like, or what the seasons were. She had forgotten that the

19

ground felt differently under your feet depending on whether it was baked hot by the sun, or soggy with rain, or crisp with frost. Today the thin mist felt cool and wet on her face; the trees were turning yellow. It was Autumn. The ground was soggy after a week of fog and rain. It squelched when Alwena moved her feet, but she managed to reach the Parson's Bridge without slipping, prodding her stick carefully through layers of wet fallen leaves.

She stood on the bridge and looked down at the fast-running river which dashed along the rocky gorge below her. This river emerged from the woods which covered the top end of the valley. It marked the boundary of the land known as Parc y Plas, fifty acres of grazing dotted with oak trees, said to be the remains of an eighteenth century landscape garden.

Beyond the parkland nothing could be seen but woods and mountains. The woods were said to be full of secret walks and gardens, shady grottoes and hidden waterfalls, long since swamped by bracken and rhododendrons or replanted with spruce and larch trees by the Forestry Commission. Alwena was always being warned not to venture into the woods, in case she got lost, or fell into the river and was swept away.

The one thing Alwena knew about the mysterious Child was that one of those secret gardens had been made especially for her. A hidden refuge in the woods all to herself.

Alwena thought about this garden a great deal. She imagined roses growing, and primroses in the spring, and a summerhouse and the Child sitting there and the birds flying down to feed from her hand. One day soon, when she was well enough, Alwena intended to disobey her parents, and set forth into the woods to find it.

*   *   *

Alwena prodded carefully up the steps at the front of Plas Idaleg and leaned against the high mahogany door so that it opened just wide enough for her to slide through into the vast entrance hall with its stone pillars and high vaulted ceiling. Far above her head a couple of birds swooped agitatedly about, darting against the glass of the tall pointed windows as they tried to escape. A gust of wind caught the door and pushed it further open, bringing with it a shower of fallen leaves which blew round Alwena's ankles and slithered across the black-and-white marble floor.

The library was at the end of one of the draughty passages which led off the hall, away from the sun in the north west corner of the house. It was called the Octagon Library because it had eight walls, lined with book-cases. It had pink marble columns and a high ceiling rising to a dome with windows round the sides. On the walls between the bookcases were painted panels on which traces of colour and gilding could just be made out under the dust of decades.

The bookcases had been empty for fifty years, but news of the restoration project was getting about, and, as T. J. Mostyn put it, Plas Idaleg had suddenly become *the* place to which to donate your grandfather's library of nineteenth-century sermons. As a result the library was now piled high with boxes and cartons of books, all of which had to be opened and unpacked and sorted in case they contained anything useful or valuable. Both Alwena's father and T. J. grumbled about this task while enjoying it mightily.

It seemed that the latest batch of books contained little to get excited about.

'You'd think the Rodericks could have done better than this,' her father was saying. 'Considering it was their house once.'

'Sir Vernon's books probably went to Sotheby's generations ago,' replied T. J. 'This is all the old stuff they couldn't get rid of anywhere else. I have to say, knowing the Rodericks, I'm not surprised.'

Sir Vernon Roderick had owned the Plas in the nineteenth century. It was he who had built the Italian-style tower. His fortune came from the lead and silver mines of Cardiganshire; his own, said T. J. Mostyn, and other people's. Sir Vernon Roderick, said T. J., had been known as the Wickedest Man in Wales. T. J. Mostyn knew all about everything that had ever happened in Wales. Alwena's brother said he was so old, he had probably lived through it all. 'He taught history to the Knights of the Round Table,' David would say. 'He helped Owain Glyndŵr get away. Lloyd George *gave* him that suit.' In a hundred years' time, thought Alwena, he'll be telling the Martians about the Morgan family who came to Plas Idaleg in the nineteen-nineties and saved it from falling down. And he'd look exactly the same as he did now, with that high wrinkled forehead and wispy hair and ash from his pipe all over his sleeves, and those shrewd old eyes faded by the light of centuries.

'Sir Vernon went in for books by the yard,' T. J. was

saying, coughing as he frowned over dusty bundles of old journals tied up with string and piles of ancient books with split bindings and yellow pages. 'It was all show with him, not like his predecessor, Edward Jones-Mortimer. Now there was a collector for you. The manuscripts! The bindings! What a tragedy that fire was. The finest library in Wales, burnt to ashes. You could see the flames in Rhayader, they say.'

'And not properly insured,' agreed Alwena's father, busy with another carton.

'But was he daunted? No he was not. He set about rebuilding the whole house—bankrupted him, of course. Broke his heart, and then of course the—' T. J. caught sight of Alwena and broke off. 'Well now, Alwena, have you come to help us?'

Alwena smiled and nodded. Her father said, 'That's very thoughtful of you, Alwena,' in a proud tone of voice which irritated her intensely. I said I was going to come and help, she thought.

'Good,' said T. J. 'That's what we want. Volunteers.'

'The more the merrier,' said her father heartily, although Alwena knew he did not mean it. He was good at sounding delighted when people offered to help with Plas Idaleg, but never taking them up on it. He wanted to keep Plas Idaleg to himself, his family and T. J. as long as possible.

'We can't have you lifting a lot of heavy books just yet, Alwena,' said T. J. 'But we can surely find something you can do.' He was piling books into his arms as he spoke, one after another out of a carton on the floor, and heaving them onto one of the bookshelves.

'Ew, my knees! When it comes to lifting, Roscoe, I'm past my best.' Holding his back, he reached for a chair and sat down, panting hoarsely. 'I'm an old man, Alwena.'

'Older than Merlin, David says,' said Alwena with a shy smile.

T. J. laughed. 'He's a character, your brother. We could do with him today, mind, to help with all this lifting. Indeed a big strapping lad like him is just what we need.'

'David,' said Alwena's father, 'would be more trouble than he's worth, the mood he's in these days.'

'I dare say,' agreed T. J. cheerfully. 'But I tell you what, Roscoe, I've got a good idea. This A Level History group I'm bringing along to visit the Plas next weekend is full of big strapping boys. Girls too. It wouldn't do them any harm to give up a few weekends to help us with a bit of sorting out and cataloguing.'

Alwena's smile disappeared. What A Level History group?

'A Level History group?' said her father.

'We did discuss it,' said T. J. with a smile.

'Oh yes,' said Alwena's father, his reluctance showing all over his face. 'I forgot.' He opened an old book and began to study it closely to avoid looking at Alwena.

This was the first she had heard of people from school coming to Plas Idaleg. People from a strange school, what was more. How could her father let T. J. talk him into allowing it and then not tell her? I'm not having people from that school coming here, she thought. She was about to say so aloud, but the twinkle in T. J.'s eye stopped her somehow.

24

'When are they coming?' she asked. She had to know, so that she could make sure she was well hidden away before they arrived.

'Next Saturday,' said T. J. 'I'd hoped it could be this week, but I couldn't get the school minibus. All this sport, you know. It'll be nice for you to see some young people of your own age again, Alwena.'

'Yes,' said Alwena furiously. Forgetting her offer of help, she snatched her stick and limped away through the house to where Bedwyr was loitering at the bottom of the front steps.

'It's a plot,' she told him. 'It's a plot to get me used to people from school, so I shan't mind going back.'

It was obviously her mother's idea. She had talked T. J. into it. It was clear her father didn't like the idea at all.

A Level people meant older people too. Boys. They would stare at her. The girls would nudge each other. Why could her mother never understand how unbearable it was to be stared at like an animal in the zoo?

Well, they won't see me, thought Alwena. I'll be hiding. I'll find the Child's Garden. That's where I'll hide.

Chapter Two

'Plas Idyllic, I don't think,' said Gareth Lloyd's father, wiping a crust of bread in the gravy on his plate and stuffing it into his mouth. 'Plas White Elephant, more like. The place should have been pulled down years ago.'

'It would do good if they restored it,' retorted his wife. 'It would bring employment.' Gareth had never once heard his father make a remark without being immediately contradicted by his mother. He exchanged here-we-go-again looks with his two younger brothers. They put their heads down and continued gobbling their evening meal. The portable television on the kitchen unit, broadcasting the Welsh news, moved on from the possible restoration of Plas Idaleg to sport, but for once Mr Lloyd was not to be side-tracked.

'It's all to do with the past,' he said. 'What about the future? That's what I say. That old house has brought nothing but trouble from the time it was built. It's swallowed up fortunes. All the lead, all the silver in these hills has gone to keep the place going, and now it wants more. More millions out of the pockets of ordinary people.'

'Fools that choose to gamble!'

'When I think of how we struggle to keep our schools open—our swimming pool. They can find millions to restore a stately home, but they can't find a few thousand to give us a decent sports centre. They couldn't even keep the local radio station going!'

'I'm not surprised,' said Gareth. 'It was rubbish.'

'Well we all know it wasn't trendy enough for *you*.'

'Male voice choirs and the Three Tenors! You're dead right.'

'Snooty little sod,' said Gareth's father. 'I don't know where he gets it from. This Plas Whatever-they're-going to-call-it will be right up his street. Full of jumped-up gasbags and intellectuals.'

26

Gareth said, 'T. J. Mostyn is all in favour of it.'

T. J. Mostyn had taught history to both his parents, and very likely their parents too.

'Well then!' said Gareth's mother. 'T. J. Mostyn is a very learned man, they say. He could have been a Professor.'

'Old and mad by now, it stands to reason,' said Gareth's father. 'You'd think they'd pension him off. Mind you, he knew his stuff, I'll give him that. He took us down a lead mine once. There was a big row about it, because of the insurance.'

'You mean, if one of the kids had fallen down a mine-shaft,' said Gareth's fourteen-year-old brother Dewi, 'nobody would have minded, so long as they were insured.' He and twelve-year-old Iestyn began to laugh loudly through mouthfuls of pudding. They had pink, freckled faces and boiling heads of curly ginger hair like their father, in contrast to Gareth who had inherited his mother's fair colouring.

'I'd have insured you two,' said Mrs Lloyd. 'I could have had a good holiday on the proceeds. Stop that, Iestyn, this is a clean table-cloth. Both of you stop messing about, you'll be late for football practice. Leave Gareth in peace to do his homework.'

Leave me in peace, full stop, thought Gareth. Sod the homework. He had taken on four A Level subjects and it wore him out just to think of them. Aloud he said, 'T. J. Mostyn wants us to go to that Plas place this weekend.'

'Oh, he does, does he?' said Mr Lloyd. 'And who's *we* when we're at home?'

'Our A Level History group. Year Twelve.'

'I can't get used to these new class numbers,' said Gareth's mother. 'Why can't they say the Sixth Form like they always used to?'

'He wants us to do a project on it for our exam. A paper.'

'Good,' said Mr Lloyd. 'You write a project on it, my boy, and don't get swept away by any propaganda nor any arty-farty stuff about the architecture. You go and see those marble halls, and ask yourself how many people died so the place could be built.'

'Any mine shafts for him to fall down?' asked Dewi. 'Better make sure he's insured, Mam.'

'No mine shafts,' said Mr Lloyd with a grin. 'There's a tower, though. I've seen it for myself. A great high tower for him to fall off.'

'Well, I'll tell T. J. you want me to say it should be pulled down,' said Gareth.

'You do that.'

'Don't listen to your father,' said Mrs Lloyd. 'If they get this money from the Lottery, they'll need plumbers up at Plas Idaleg, sure to. Hot water and central heating is the first thing they'll want, and if he's not there with his estimates at the head of the queue I shall want to know the reason why. Anyway,' she added, 'you know you'd never be able to keep away. You're that nosy.'

'It'll never happen,' said Mr Lloyd. He stood up from the kitchen table, unhooked his jacket from the back of the kitchen door and put it on over his track suit. He was the coach for the Under 16s football team of which both Dewi and Iestyn were members. 'I said I'd call at the Miners Arms afterwards, to look at their glass-washing machine,' he told his wife. At the open door he paused and looked back at Gareth. 'That Plas,' he said, 'there used to be a queer old story about when it was first built. Something about a child. You want to ask them about it.'

*   *   *

At nine o'clock on Saturday morning Gareth was waiting with the seven other members of the A Level History group outside the main doors of Abercoed High School waiting for the school minibus to pick them up for the eight mile journey north to Plas Idaleg. They huddled against the wall to protect themselves from the rain which swept horizontally across the playground, blown in from the coast ten miles to the west.

'This place we're going to,' said Elin Davies, huddling inside her inadequate leather jacket. 'It has got a roof, hasn't it?' She shot a flirtatious sideways glance at Gareth, and his heart sank a little.

'It must have, or the books would get rained on,' said Llŷr Thomas, who was called Llŷr Hir because he was so tall.

'T. J. wouldn't allow that,' said Elin's friend Gwenno, who was Llŷr's on-and-off girlfriend and nearly as tall as he was. 'He wouldn't allow a book to get rained on. Human beings, though, it doesn't matter about them.'

The minibus arrived, splashing through the puddles on the uneven tarmac. ('Terrible drainage,' was Gareth's father's opinion. 'The whole surface wants taking up and re-laying.') Gareth jostled himself on board at the head of the group in order to claim one of the front seats behind the driver. He liked journeys: you never knew

29

what might be at the end of them, and he liked to look out at where he was going. Not that there was much to see today in all this rain. The mountains were invisible and it was barely light.

'What do you think it will be like?' asked Elin, sitting down next to him and stuffing her bag, which was full of packets of crisps and cans of Coke, on the floor between them. Gareth remembered uneasily that he had ended up snogging her at the disco last night, so no doubt she now regarded herself as his girlfriend.

'Dad says there's a tower.'

'I knew about the tower. Childe Somebody to the Dark Tower Came,' said Elin. 'My Mam keeps saying that. It's a poem or something. And what's that other one, something about a stately pleasure dome, we did it in English.'

'Well then, it must be some kind of stately home, I suppose.'

He had visited a few stately homes with his parents, or on school trips. Powis Castle, for example, his mother loved the gardens there, and that place on Anglesey. Then they had been to Cardiff and seen Cardiff Castle and those big buildings in Cathays Park. Not that you could call them stately homes exactly, although the Museum did have a grand flight of steps up to the entrance, and stone pillars like some palace out of a Disney film.

Gareth liked big buildings, without really knowing why. He spent a lot of time drawing them with the mouse on his computer. There weren't many in this part of Cardiganshire, not that you could call really large, apart

30

from the Hospital. This was a great square, plain brick building that old people in Abercoed called the Workhouse, which was what it had originally been. They spoke of it with loathing and said it should have been pulled down years ago, but the way the world was going, they'd all end up back there before very long. Despite its sinister reputation, Gareth liked this building too.

The minibus chugged across the mountain road, buffeted by the wind and rain. There were no villages on this bleak upland, just sheep and a few isolated farms. Occasionally they passed the tumbledown remains of an abandoned lead mine, perhaps a few roofless stone sheds with collapsing walls, a broken-down chimney or a derelict water-wheel. What did they look like when they were first built, Gareth wondered. Who had built them? Who had worked in them?

'What happened to all the people who worked in the lead mines?' he said aloud. 'There must have been hundreds of people. When you look at all the old workings all over the place.'

'Gone,' said Penry Jones, the young History teacher who was driving the minibus. 'Gone to South Wales. Gone to Liverpool. Gone back to Ireland. Gone back to Italy, some of them.'

'I wish I could go back to Italy,' said Elin. 'It might be a bit warmer.' She snuggled up to Gareth with a coy smile.

'Well, you're going to the Italian House,' said Penry. 'Plas Idaleg. That'll have to do you for now.'

'Plas Idyllic, they call it in English, my Dad says,' said Gareth, edging forward in his seat so that Elin could not lean against him.

The road suddenly began to descend steeply and Penry changed gear. The wind dropped and the rain abated a little. Ahead of them lay more hills covered with conifer plantations and the occasional patch of mixed woodland. At the bottom of the hill the road turned sharply, crossed a stone bridge thickly overgrown with ivy, and continued through a village of small grey houses crouched up against the edge of the forest. 'Look out for a set of iron gates and a stone lodge house, T. J. said,' Penry instructed over his shoulder. 'Hullo, this looks like it.'

'No gates, only gateposts,' said Gareth.

'He probably remembers when there *were* gates.'

'Isn't it dark?' said Elin. 'Is that T. J.'s house? He must have to have the lights on all day.'

'They say he never goes to bed,' said Llŷr Hir. 'He sits up in a chair all night long reading old Welsh manuscripts.'

'He's got asthma,' said Penry.

The minibus jolted along a stony unmade road full of puddles, and overhung with the branches of oak and birch and hazel trees. Long tendrils of ivy and brambles scraped the bus windows as Penry negotiated it round the worst potholes.

'Look at the trees,' said Elin. 'It's like Sleeping Beauty, and we've got to hack our way in through the undergrowth to rescue her from the Wicked Witch.'

'No hacking needed,' said Penry. 'I see light ahead.' A few moments later the minibus crossed a cattle grid and left the woods behind. The wind and rain hit it at full force, nearly forcing it off the road. Penry braked hard and the engine stalled. The A Level History group lurched forward and stared out through the windscreen.

Oh my God, thought Gareth. It is huge. Oh my God.

'*Uffern!*' whispered Elin. 'Look at that! Dracula's castle!'

'It's not a castle,' said someone else. 'It's a palace.'

'No, it's a church, look at those pointed windows.'

'What? A cathedral, more like. And what's that funny-shaped turret?'

'Wow!' said Penry Jones. 'I knew it was big, but I didn't know it was this big. No wonder the University didn't want to take it on.'

'I don't like it,' said Elin. 'It's spooky.'

'Full of vampires,' said someone else with a giggle. 'Keep your necks covered, folks.'

'Full of red kites, anyway,' said Penry, looking up. 'They'll have us, if the vampires don't.'

Penry started the minibus again and drove the last few yards to the entrance of the house. They all jumped out and ran through the rain up the steps to the open front doors.

Gareth hung back to gaze at the house, trying to comprehend its scale. He felt it was looking back at him. He wished he were there on his own to look and look at the house without idiots like Elin making stupid remarks.

'Come on, Gareth, you'll get soaked!'

Slowly he followed the others, pausing at the top of the steps to touch the carved stone of the arched doorway. Little furry patches of lichen grew in the crevices, orange and silver and pinkish green. He rubbed his thumb against them, and felt the cold of the stone underneath.

*   *   *

'Colonnades and conservatories, cloisters and campaniles,' said T. J. Mostyn, smiling his almost toothless smile at the A Level History group. 'You'll find them all here. And don't you tell me, Gwenno Jones, that you don't know what a campanile is.' He pronounced it campan*ee*ly.

'Bell tower,' snapped Gwenno. 'Campanology, bell-ringing. Therefore campan*ee*ly, bell tower.' She was doing A Level Music as well as History.

'It's different,' said Gareth. 'It's a different shape from the rest of the house. Sort of square.'

'Quite right,' said T. J. 'Built sixty years later than the original house might have something to do with it, by our old friend Sir Vernon Roderick, in the Italianate style. Whereas the original part of the house is what you might call Gothic. Gothick with a k on the end in English, now why do you think that is?'

Nobody could guess.

'It's freezing cold in here,' Elin whispered to Gareth. 'I'm dying for a coffee.'

'I thought only cathedrals were Gothic,' said Gareth. 'Medieval, and that.'

'This is like that anyway,' said Gwenno. 'Look at the ceiling.' They craned their necks back to look at the vaulted ceiling.

'The Gothic style became fashionable again in the eighteenth century,' lectured T. J. 'It was felt to

34

complement the romantic landscape. This was the Age of the Picturesque. You should know all this, Gareth, if you want to be an architect.'

Gareth cursed the day he had mentioned this ambition to the careers teacher. It seemed to have gone right round the school. It wasn't even as if he was serious. Anyway, you couldn't build houses like this one nowadays, covered with stone carving and fancy windows and battlements; it was all concrete tower blocks as his father was always reminding him.

Gareth could not concentrate on T. J.'s lecture about the house and the man who had built it and where the money had come from. He felt rather drunk. That Italian tower would make a good block of flats, he thought. He began to re-design it in his head, adding more windows and balconies and re-siting it on a city river bank. London, he thought. Paris. Rome. The names of cities began to roll through his head like a mantra. Sydney. New York. Kuala Lumpar. Venice. Vladivostok.

'Right,' said T. J. 'Any questions before we start? Gareth?'

Gareth jumped. He glared at T. J., trying to remember the questions his father had told him to ask about whether houses like this were a good thing or not.

'All right. We'll start in the library. Follow me!'

T. J. might be ancient, but slow he was not. He led the group at a fast pace along a series of dark, lofty passages lined with massive closed doors. The passages smelled damp; they turned and turned on themselves like a maze. The heavily carved doors looked as though they had been closed for centuries. It was like being in a video game.

35

To get out of the maze you had to open one of the doors, but only one of them led to fresh air and freedom. Behind all the others, dungeons and dragons lay in wait. Gareth loitered behind the others, letting the doors challenge him. He counted out ten paces, then grasped the nearest door knob. As his fingers closed round the door knob a dog began to bark fiercely. The door knob vibrated with the sound of the barking. Gareth snatched his hand away as though he had been bitten and the barking stopped.

Gareth's skin crept. He listened for a moment, not daring to look round. He stared at the door knob as though waiting for it to bark at him again. Some dead leaves rustled round his feet, but there was no other sound. Stupid. Just some dog barking outside, that was all. All the same, he could not bring himself to try the door again. You great wimp, he told himself as he hurried after the others.

They had arrived in a dark panelled hall with a curved staircase which rose to a gallery. Light filtered in through a half-open door which appeared to lead to a sort of glassed-in terrace or conservatory.

Gareth slid into the group between Llŷr and Elin. 'Did you hear that dog?' he hissed.

'What dog?'

The dog barked again, fainter this time, not outside though; possibly upstairs. A long way off, a sort of tapping, or shuffling, could be heard, not quite footsteps. A door banged shut. Elin began to shiver and look over her shoulder. 'It's dead spooky in here, isn't it,' she whispered. 'I wouldn't like to be here on my own at night. Anything could happen!'

'It's just the wind,' said Llŷr.

'It can't be,' said Gwenno. 'You can't hear the wind and the rain in here at all. The walls must be so thick.'

T. J. Mostyn glanced upward as though he knew all about the dog and the noises. He pulled an old metal pocket watch from his waistcoat pocket and looked at the time. 'Right,' he said. 'This is the library. In you come, now.'

They followed him into the eight-sided room. The girls gave loud sighs of relief as they realised that it was warm. Gareth hung back by the door, looking out towards the staircase. He could have sworn he heard footsteps. A scraping, scuffling noise again, and that odd tapping. But then it was quiet.

'When you're ready, Gareth,' said T. J.

'Sorry,' muttered Gareth.

'I want to thank Mr Roscoe Morgan for welcoming us to Plas Idaleg today, and to introduce him to you all. Mr Roscoe Morgan is the Warden of Plas Idaleg, and another old pupil of Ysgol Abercoed, I'm pleased to say.'

Mr Roscoe Morgan was a dark, slimly built man with skin drawn tightly over the bones of his face and deep-set, restless eyes. He did not look as though he was wild to welcome people from his old school to Plas Idaleg. He looked about the same age as Gareth's father. Would they remember one another? I bet they didn't get on, thought Gareth.

Roscoe Morgan began to tell them the same stuff about the history of the house that they had already heard from T. J. Gareth let it wash over him as he gazed round the library. There was something deeply pleasing about the proportions of the walls and the marble columns and the high circular ceiling, which rose to a round, dome-shaped window through which the daylight poured. It was a pity the place was in such a mess, with all these piles of tatty old books everywhere.

'That window in the roof is called a lantern,' said Roscoe Morgan, seeing Gareth gazing upwards.

'He knows that, don't you, Gareth,' said T. J. 'He's interested in architecture.'

'Oh good,' said Roscoe Morgan. 'Please ask any questions you want.' The usual silence fell on the group. He looked at his watch, then over his shoulder. Behind him, two slender windows between the bookcases looked across a patch of grass to the woods. A donkey grazed by the hedge.

'Well, come on, someone,' said T. J. 'Elin? Gwenno?'

'Can you climb up the campan*eely*?' asked Gwenno at last, drawing out the last syllable of the word with an ironic glance at T. J.

'It's not safe at the moment,' replied Mr Morgan with a faint relaxation of his expression. 'The stairs have collapsed, so it's boarded up. But we hope to restore it, if we get the Lottery money.'

'Some people,' said Gareth carefully, 'think it's wrong to spend millions of pounds on an old house in the middle of nowhere.' He shifted from one foot to the other, not looking at anyone. 'Because of the homeless, and all that.'

Well, Dad, you can't say I didn't ask, he thought.

'Gareth likes to play Devil's Advocate sometimes,' said T. J., clapping Gareth jovially on the shoulder.

'People have no sense of history nowadays,' said Mr Morgan. 'All right, flatten Plas Idaleg and build flats for the homeless. Why not flatten all the other great houses and castles in Wales as well while we're at it? After all, what does history—what does heritage matter? Pull it all down, why not?'

'Yeah, why not,' muttered Llŷr Hir.

'I'm only saying what some people think,' said Gareth. 'I'm not saying I think it should be pulled down. I wouldn't mind coming here myself, if I was an architecture student.'

'If I was one of the homeless I wouldn't want to come here anyway,' said Elin. 'It's too cold.'

Mr Morgan joined in the laughter that followed this remark but his eyes flickered angrily from Elin to Gareth. He seemed about to speak again when Penry Jones interjected tactfully, 'Perhaps you could tell us a bit more about the agricultural improvements made by the first owner of Plas Idaleg, Mr Morgan. There's quite an emphasis on economic history now in the A Level syllabus.'

'Perhaps you could show us the stables and the model dairy, Roscoe,' suggested T. J.

'Well, it's rather wild outside. And this young lady is feeling the cold.' Mr Morgan smiled archly at Elin, and coughed. Suddenly he looked up, past them, as though something had caught his eye. Gareth turned round, and saw only the open door into the hallway. But there went that dog again, barking like mad, not far away at all. And afterwards he could not be quite sure whether or not he had seen a small head, bobbing out of sight behind the bannisters.

*   *   *

'That is the coldest place I have ever been in my life,' said Elin as they boarded the minibus for the journey home at four o'clock that afternoon.

'Good place for a rave, though,' shouted Gwenno, leaping up the steps behind them. 'You could fix up a brilliant PA in that campane*ely!*'

'Not at this time of year you couldn't. And if T. J. thinks he's going to press-gang me along there every Saturday he's got another think coming.'

Good, thought Gareth. I can come on my own and get on with some work. He envisaged himself standing at just the right distance from the house, pencil and cartridge pad in hand, drawing the place. A project for his A Level Art it could be. And it would annoy that Roscoe Morgan as well. Into another shot on his mental computer screen came the library, and the piles of old journals about the history of Cardiganshire that T. J. had asked him to sort out according to title and year of publication. The earliest ones dated from before the First World War, their pages brown and flaky with age. The sequence was complete except for a volume from the 1950s. Gareth had hunted for it through several other piles of journals, without success.

'It was supposed to be a complete set,' said Roscoe Morgan. 'The *Transactions*, and then *Ceredigion*. I can't think what can have happened. Oh well—I suppose it isn't the end of the world.' But he spoke fretfully, glaring at Gareth as though it were his fault.

He didn't want us there really, thought Gareth. He hated it. He kept on looking over his shoulder all the time as though he was wishing it was time for us to go.

'You made yourself popular,' said Llŷr Hir, leaning over from the seat behind. 'Asking all those questions about people dying in the lead mines while they were spending fortunes on building that house. Had you been reading it up, or what?'

'My Dad was going on about it,' said Gareth. 'It'll be the first thing he asks me when I get home.'

'He liked the place really, didn't you, Gareth,' said Gwenno. 'It's right up your street, all that architecture.'

'You've got to look at all sides of the picture.'

'That Mr Morgan looked as though he wanted to hit you over the head. T. J. was laughing, I saw him. Then when you stuck your hand up to volunteer to help in that library again next week—his face—talk about sick—'

'Yeah,' said Gareth, plugging his Walkman into his ears to encourage Llŷr to sit down and shut up. He wanted to go back to thinking about the house. He anchored his bag between his feet, thinking of the old large-scale Ordnance Survey map covering Plas Idaleg and its immediate surroundings, which lay hidden there between the pages of his computer magazine. Just a loan, he thought. I'll take it back next time. I'll get it photocopied.

Gareth had come across the map among another pile of old journals and was still pleased with himself for appropriating it so coolly under the very nose of Mr Roscoe Morgan. Serve him right, he thought, for being so snotty.

Chapter Three

'That one with the long hair,' said Alwena's father. 'That Gareth. I shall have to have a word with T. J. I don't like the look of him.'

Alwena had never known her father so agitated. He could not leave the subject alone.

'The worst kind of little know-all,' he said. 'Flats for the homeless indeed!'

'They are Sixth-Formers,' said Alwena's mother. 'They are supposed to ask intelligent questions.' She was moving round the kitchen, making supper. Alwena was sitting by the kitchen range in her wheelchair. She had lasted until the minibus had left, then her legs had given out. It was her own fault, for spying on the Sixth-Formers all day. She had not been able to resist, especially as her resolution to go searching for the Child's Garden had been thwarted by the weather.

But it had been exciting, spying on the visitors, like keeping the enemy under surveillance. Especially that Gareth, with his long hair straight and blond as a Viking's, who had never stopped staring at everything and asking awkward questions. She was on her father's side against the marauders one hundred per cent, and furious with her mother for being so calm about them.

'He was being provocative, the little so-and-so. I could see it in his face. They were all the same, no understanding of the place, no sensitivity. This precious collection of books we're building up, it meant nothing to them. We can't have people about the place who don't even respect books.'

'Oh come on, Roscoe, you said yourself most of the donations are rubbish. You should be grateful that you've got some help for a week or two. Besides, it'll be nice to have a few fresh young faces about the place. It'll be good for Alwena too.'

'I don't want them here,' said Alwena, folding her arms around herself and shrinking into her chair.

'You see?' said her father. 'Look at the state she's in. She's stressed out.'

'Just because some poor lad has upset *you*.' Alwena's mother pushed a bowl of salad into her husband's hands. He took it silently and put it on the table. Rather sulkily he began to lay out plates and cutlery.

'If he's one of those boys of Lloyd the plumber I know what he's like,' he said after a moment. 'I remember his father at school and a hot-tempered, argumentative so-and-so he was too. Always in trouble.'

'Oh! I see; the sins of the fathers. That's hardly fair, now, is it?'

'What I'm saying is, what respect is a boy like that going to have for historic books? He couldn't even put a set of journals into date order without losing some. That was definitely a full set of *Ceredigion*, it was on the inventory. We'll have to find the missing volume.'

'Roscoe, you can pick up odd volumes of *Ceredigion* in any second-hand bookshop. Besides, the inventory might have been wrong. I doubt very much whether the executors would have checked every single item.'

'Well, I shall talk to T. J.,' said Alwena's father obstinately. 'It's a matter of priorities here and my main concern is Alwena.'

'Oh yes, of course, Alwena.'

Oh yes, of course, Alwena! thought Alwena indignantly. She doesn't care about me nearly as much as Dad, she thought. She *wants* boys to come here and stare at me and cause trouble in the library. She glared at her memory of the boy called Gareth. He had a middle parting like the pop stars on the covers of the teenage magazines her parents did not allow her to read. She had watched from the upper landing as he gazed dreamily about and T. J. shouted at him to pay attention, and she had been outside the library door when he had suddenly woken up from his reverie and started talking about the homeless. Olwen hated him already too, she wouldn't stop barking and Alwena had had to drag her upstairs and shut her in a distant bedroom.

He had obviously only volunteered to help in the library to cause trouble. In fact he was probably just the kind of person who would have stolen that missing copy of *Ceredigion*.

If it had not already been taken by Alwena herself, days ago, and hidden at the bottom of her very deepest bedroom drawer.

*   *   *

It must have fallen out of one of the cartons of books when they were being unpacked. Alwena had noticed it one day when she had been alone in the library revising her French lesson. It had been another of her good days and she had been pleased with herself for being able to bend down and pick it up without any help.

The journal had not looked particularly interesting,

but flicking through the pages Alwena's attention had been caught by the title of one of the articles. 'A Walk around the Gardens at Plas Idaleg.' In smaller print underneath it said, 'Reprinted from *Cambrian Countryside Notes*, Vol XLIII, 1853'. On the facing page was an illustration, an old-fashioned black and white engraving of woods and rocks and a waterfall. Underneath the picture was written, in funny sloping type, 'The Pensile Garden at Plas Idaleg: known as the Child's Garden.'

The Child's Garden.

It must have been meant. It must have fallen in that particular place especially so that she could find it.

With racing heart, Alwena had stuffed the journal out of sight between the pages of her French exercise book before either of her parents returned.

It was essential that her parents did not know of her discovery. They would certainly find some excuse for whisking the journal away and making sure she never saw it again. She would have to smuggle it up to her bedroom, so that she could read the article and possibly copy it out before putting it back in the library, where with luck it would be filed with the other issues of *Ceredigion* and never looked at again.

The problem was how to do all this in secret. Alwena was not in the habit of spending time in her bedroom; her father said it was too cold. Anyway the evenings were getting quite dark now and if her parents saw her bedroom light on they would come in to see what she was doing.

Trying to work out how to get round this had

preoccupied Alwena all week. She had been unable to replace the borrowed journal before Saturday, when the terrible invasion of Gareth and his friends had led to its loss being discovered. She felt guilty and furious at the same time. It served them right if her father believed one of them had stolen the journal; if they had not come he would not have been able to do so. If they had not come, nobody would ever have missed it in the first place.

*   *   *

As soon as she awoke on Sunday morning Alwena knew it was going to be a bad day. Her joints were hot and swollen and her legs would hardly move. As she lay in bed her feet twitched in a spasm of cramp which sent daggers of pain through her ankles. She knew what this meant: a day confined to her wheelchair, just when she had hoped to find an hour to slip quietly away to her room to read the article. It would have been her best chance for ages, with her mother cooking Sunday lunch and her father busy in the library with T. J.

It was hard not to weep with pain and frustration. Why did she have to have a bad day *today*? Just when she wanted to be really well so that no-one would fuss over her and tell her to keep warm and not to go off on her own in case she fell over.

It was all the fault of those Sixth Formers. If she had not had to watch them she would not have worn herself out, straining her joints as she bent to hide behind the bannisters.

Alwena lay in bed, raging against Gareth and his friends. She'd never be able to do anything while they were coming to the house. There was the journal hidden in her chest of drawers not two yards away, and she was too weak to get out of bed to read what it had to say about the Child's garden.

Well, she would be blowed if she would let them beat her. She had to read that article, bad day or no bad day.

The cramp in her feet had woken Alwena early; it was getting light but the house was still Sunday quiet. She began to do her ankle exercises, clenching her teeth against the pain and rubbing her knees a little to warm them up. Listening carefully for sounds of movement from her parents' room she struggled upright and edged her legs carefully to the side of the bed, shivering and swallowing to suppress helpless whimpers of pain. If she could just stand for long enough to reach across to her bedroom chair she could support herself between it and the chest of drawers.

She made it with a stagger, saving herself against the chest of drawers and leaning on it to rest her throbbing knees. Her heart was nearly bursting with the effort of not crying out. Her face in the mirror which stood on top of the chest was gaunt and pale, her short dark hair sticking out all over her head from being slept on. Her eyes were swollen with tears of pain which she wiped away with the sleeve of her nightdress.

Oh, she was ugly. Stunted and ugly.

Those Sixth Formers who came yesterday would be, what was it, Year Twelve, sixteen, perhaps seventeen years old. Barely two years older than she was, yet they were twice her size, even the girls.

Alwena hated them. She hated them for being tall and

beautiful, and for laughing and grumbling about the cold and pretending they were trapped in Dracula's castle, as though Plas Idaleg was a great joke. They were so noisy, even worse than her brother David. They filled the house with their noise. Alwena could still hear it rattling away in her head. They had made her feel like a small black spider scrabbling frantically about the place to find a hole to hide in.

Alwena took a deep breath, shifting her arms on the chest of drawers. Never mind about that now. The article. She would have to bend down to open the drawer. Her legs wavered and trembled. Cautiously she reached out for the chair, which was a lightweight one made of wicker, and pulled it across the rug. She almost collapsed into it, shaking with fatigue.

She righted herself and rested for a few moments, pressing her fingers against her knuckles in her habitual gesture. All was still silent in the house. She wiped her face on the sleeve of her nightdress once more, then bent forward and took hold of the handles of the drawer in which she had hidden the journal.

The chest of drawers was modern; it had been deliberately chosen so that Alwena could manage it, with light drawers which opened and closed smoothly and handles that were easy to grip. This morning the drawer flew open so easily it hit Alwena on the shins and she nearly fainted from the pain and the effort of not crying aloud.

When her thumping heart had quieted sufficiently for her to hear that her parents still did not seem to have woken up, she bent forward again and removed the journal from under the pile of sweaters where she had hidden it. She rearranged the sweaters to make a little space for the journal so that she could read it without taking it out of the drawer. If either of her parents came in they would think she was merely looking for something to wear, and she could push the journal out of sight very quickly before they noticed.

Alwena took a series of deep breaths, pleased with herself for working out this strategy. Suddenly she was filled with exhilaration at having made her body do something it had not wanted to do. On a bad day, the kind of day when she would hitherto have lain in bed until her father came in to lift her into her wheelchair, she had got out of bed and walked across her room, on her own. The pain, her body's revenge, was awful. But it was worth it.

Alwena stared wildly at herself in the mirror for a moment, then opened the journal and began to read.

*   *   *

'Did you ask about what I said?' shouted Gareth's father from underneath his van on Sunday morning, as Gareth bent to leave a mug of tea on the ground within reach.

'Yes!' Gareth shouted back.

Gareth's father wriggled out from underneath the van and sat up with a grin. He wiped his hands on an oily rag and picked up his tea. 'And what did they say?'

'T. J. said I was being the Devil's Advocate.'

'Well he would, crafty old bugger.'

'The other guy didn't like it,' said Gareth. 'The one that lives there. Morgan, his name was. Roscoe Morgan. He went to our school, T. J. said.'

'Morgan,' said Gareth's father. 'Who would that be then? How old was he?'

'Older than you. Not much though. Thin.'

'Thin. *Uffern*, who would that be? You wouldn't expect a local there, somehow. County type, English, you'd have thought. Whaddyou think of the house, then?'

Gareth decided against winding his father up too much. It was a Sunday morning after all. 'Big,' he said. 'Old. Damp.'

'It won't have a damp course,' said Gareth's father. 'They'll have to put one in if they want to do it up. That'll be a joke.'

'It was freezing cold.'

'I bet it was. The old feller who lived there before the war used to spend the winters in Aberystwyth,' said Gareth's father. 'Now, who told me that? He had two nurses. They used to wheel him up and down along the Prom.'

'I said I'd go again next week.'

'Whose idea was that, yours or T. J.'s?'

'It's for my A Level project,' said Gareth. 'They've got some books I can look at in the library.' He knew if he said, they want volunteers to *help* in the library, his father would explode. Gareth was supposed to help his father on Saturdays, to earn his allowance.

'Funny how these things all happen on a Saturday, isn't it?' His father gave him a beady, don't-think-you-can-fool-me look as he swallowed his tea and handed the mug back to Gareth.

'It's for A Levels,' repeated Gareth. 'Anyway, I'll go on my bike.'

'All this A Level business,' said his father. 'I hope it's all worth it. Just you remember what it's costing me to keep you on at school, that's all.'

Gareth said nothing, not wanting to provoke one of his father's rants about the uselessness and expense of A Levels and universities and people with letters after their name who didn't know anything about the real world.

'Take no notice,' his mother would say. 'He doesn't mean half of it. He's quick enough to pick your brain on the old maths when he needs to. And when your picture's in the paper in your cap and gown with your BA rolled up in your hand he'll be flashing it about every pub in town.'

That was all very well, but it took five years to qualify as an architect. Five years. The prospect of his father wearing that was remote, even if his grades were good enough for him to get a place at a school of architecture at all, which was unlikely.

Gareth mooched glumly to the end of the short drive and looked out at the circle of detached modern houses behind their open plan gardens. The estate stood on the edge of the town with its small grey terraces and slate roofs. Behind the town the wild Cardiganshire uplands rolled away like a desert, cutting it off from the rest of the world. The possibility of crossing that desert with a fistful of A Levels to see what lay on the other side seemed as intangible as the wind.

Meanwhile, Plas Idaleg was near, and real, and beautiful. Gareth was elated by its hugeness; it made the whole world seem bigger. If that Morgan chap ever left he'd be tempted to go and squat there. He'd take over that great big room on the ground floor that T. J. called the 'saloon' (Elin and Llŷr had sniggered and started to ask where the bar was) and put up black velvet curtains which trailed on the floor and a mattress covered with carpet and a state-of-the-art hi-fi. He'd cut wood and burn it in the huge fireplace and cook sides of lamb on a spit.

Now and again he'd hold parties. Gwenno had been right about it being a good place for a rave. But he wouldn't have anybody living with him, least of all any women. His dream collapsed from the sublime to the ridiculous as he saw himself stuck with Elin, being domestic and wanting him to get his Dad to install central heating.

Gareth saw girls like Elin in the same light as he saw his father: as people whose object was to prevent him from ever escaping from Abercoed. Girls wanted steady boyfriends and engagement rings and babies, not necessarily in that order, but all part of the same plot. Well, some girls weren't like that, Gwenno for instance; but most were.

His father's voice cut into his reverie. 'If you're going to stand there staring into space you can come and give me a hand.'

'I've got homework,' said Gareth.

'Why aren't you doing it then? Come on, you can come with me to collect those old radiators from Cambrian View and we can get it done before dinner. People pay good money for these old radiators nowadays. Architectural heritage. It ought to be right up your street.'

'Okay,' said Gareth.

"Okay',' Gareth's father mimicked his offhand tone. *'Iesu*, I wish you'd wake up a bit. You make me tired just looking at you. Talk about half-soaked.'

'It's all the sex and drugs,' said Gareth.

'I sometimes wish it were,' said his father. 'It'd be more natural.' He got into the van and slammed the door. 'Get a move on, we haven't got all day.'

After dinner Gareth left his father and brothers watching a football match on television and went up to his room. It was the third and smallest bedroom in the house and it had never seemed smaller. When he squatted at Plas Idaleg he would take over the biggest bedroom for himself as well as the saloon; he'd set up his computer in the Octagon Library and put his maps and drawing board up in another room to themselves. All that space. It wouldn't matter how cold it was, he thought, lying on his bed in his small room with its double-glazed window and its oil-fired central heating radiator turned full on.

After a while he rolled off the bed and searched his bag for the computer magazine in which he had secreted the old Ordnance Survey map out of the Plas. It was very old, and worn at the creases. He opened it carefully and laid it on his drawing board, tilting the board to get the best of the daylight.

When Gareth had seen the house yesterday it looked as though it had been dropped from the skies into that stretch of open land in the middle of the forest. It had felt as though the minibus had had to tunnel its way through the woods to reach it. The fascinating thing about this map was that it showed that ninety years ago the forest had not been anything like as thick—well, no Forestry Commission in those days, Gareth supposed vaguely—and was threaded with footpaths which seemed to link together in a designed sort of way, as though leading from viewpoint to viewpoint.

He frowned and peered to read the tiny letters in which the place names were printed, then sat back to get his bearings on the whole estate and where it was in relation to Abercoed and the lead mines and the village by the lodge house. There seemed to be no quicker or flatter route to the Plas from Abercoed than the one taken by the minibus yesterday. Gareth resigned himself to an hour's hard pedalling each way, next Saturday. He noted that the farm where Llŷr Hir lived was less than two miles from the Plas, near a map reference indicating a lead mine. Llŷr needn't have bothered to come on the bus, thought Gareth. He could have biked it.

The river flowed through the middle of the estate on a steep gradient, over what looked like at least two waterfalls. Footpaths led up to the waterfalls; Gareth imagined ladies in crinolines teetering on the edges of precipices like the ones in those old prints of Devil's Bridge belonging to his mother. With his magnifying glass he could just make out some of the names dotted about the map. *Ladies' Wk.*, said one; *Blaengarw Fm.*, said another, and another, *Child's Gdn.*

The one thing he'd forgotten to do yesterday at Plas Idaleg was to ask about the Child. Well, he hadn't really been very interested when his father had mentioned it, then what with the whole business of actually seeing the

54

place, and asking all the wrong questions of the man who looked after it, and pinching maps, he'd completely forgotten about it.

He hadn't even connected it with those weird noises and that barking dog. Now he was suddenly reminded of the small figure he felt sure he had seen on the stairs.

It would be a laugh if the place was haunted by this Child his father had talked about. A child with a barking dog.

Gareth laughed aloud. How daft could you get? But he shivered a bit as well.

Chapter Four

'If they're going to be helping you all day,' said Alwena's mother at breakfast the following Friday morning, 'the least we can do is give them lunch.'

'T. J.'s told them to bring sandwiches and a flask,' replied her father. 'He doesn't want us to be put to any expense. Anyway,' he added with a sniff, 'they'll probably prefer to be left on their own for their lunch break. They'll want to go outside and have a smoke.'

Alwena's mother said, 'Well, I can see you're going to give them a wonderful welcome.'

'I wouldn't be surprised if none of them turn up,' said her father. 'They probably only put their hands up last week because T. J. was there. I bet you they won't turn up.'

'I hope they don't,' said Alwena.

'Nonsense,' said her mother. 'It'll be fun for you.'

'They'll stare at me.'

'No they won't, Alwena. They looked a nice crowd of young people, I thought.'

Her husband snorted. 'A nice gang of little vandals, more like.'

'Roscoe, that's not fair.'

'Well, I shall have to tell the Trustees,' said Alwena's father, swallowing the last of his coffee and standing up. 'It's a good thing the meeting starts before lunch. I shall bring it up at the top of the Agenda, then I can phone T. J. if they don't think it's a good idea.'

'I suppose we know what your recommendation will be,' said his wife. 'Well, I must say, if you want my opinion I think you're being a bit silly and I bet the Trustees will as well.'

'We shall see.' Roscoe Morgan put on his coat, scarf and gloves and picked up a pile of folders labelled 'University of Wales: Plas Idaleg Trust' from the sideboard. He kissed his daughter on the cheek. 'Bye-bye, Alwena, keep warm.'

Alwena ate another finger of toast with Marmite and listened for the sound of the car driving away. Her mother began to stack plates into the sink for washing up.

Alwena said casually, 'It's quite nice out. Can I go for a little walk before I do my lessons?'

'If you like. It seems a shame to miss out on the sunshine. Do you want me to come with you? How about a ride on Bedwyr?'

'Oh no, he's so stubborn when you ride him, he won't move.'

'True.' Alwena's mother laughed.

'And you don't need to come with me, Mum, I'm feeling all right today.'

'All right, but don't be too long. I thought you might like to help me develop those pictures of the conservatory.' Mrs Morgan was keen on photography and often found ways of bringing it into Alwena's lessons.

'That would be nice.'

Mrs Morgan turned from the sink to observe her daughter for a moment or two. 'About tomorrow,' she said. 'There's nothing to worry about, you know. They're not going to eat you.'

Alwena stopped chewing, laid the uneaten stub of toast on her plate and began to work her bent fingers.

'I don't suppose more than one or two of them will turn up. It would be nice if you could meet them, don't you think? I'll take them some coffee and you could come with me. Just to say hello, so they'll know who you are if they meet you round the house.'

'I don't want to meet them.'

Her mother came and sat down in the chair next to her. 'It seems a pity to miss the chance of meeting a few people from Abercoed, in case you do start back there instead of Aber.'

'They're too big,' said Alwena.

'Seventeen year olds. That's only two years older than you. And they might have younger brothers and sisters.'

'They'll *stare* at me!'

'They won't, I promise you,' said her mother. She tried to cover Alwena's hand with her own but Alwena snatched it away and began to press her knuckles agitatedly.

'They will!' she cried. 'It's all very well for you, you don't know what it's like!'

'Alwena, you aren't going to be able to hide away from the world forever. You're growing up, you need to get back to school. Make friends! Get out and about!'

'I don't want to go back to school. I want to stay here forever.'

'Nothing lasts forever,' replied her mother, beginning to sound impatient. 'You might as well learn that now as later. Besides, Alwena, you're an intelligent girl. You owe it to yourself to start thinking about the future. You'll be starting your GCSEs next year, and you know how important they are. *I* can't prepare you for them, you need to be back in school.'

'It's not fair!' cried Alwena. 'You're getting at me. You waited on purpose until Dad was out of the way so he wouldn't be here to stick up for me.'

'Your father spoils you,' said her mother. 'It's time you started thinking things out for yourself. Facing up to the world. And if the world stares at you, so what? You'll just have to stare right back.'

'I hate you,' said Alwena. 'You're a horrible mother. I shall tell Dad what you said.' She pulled herself to her feet, ignoring her mother's helping hand. 'I'm going out and I shan't be back for *ages*.'

'Take Bedwyr with you,' said her mother, turning back to the washing up with a sigh.

Outside, a pale sun shone across the frosty landscape. Alwena pulled up the hood of her down jacket and prodded her stick into the ground. It was hard on the surface but soft underneath, like icing on a sponge cake. She looked around at the thick dark woods, trying not to cry. Her mother was so horrible, she didn't care twopence about Alwena's feelings.

I don't care, Alwena told herself. I'm going to find the Child's Garden. If I get lost, I don't care. She imagined search parties, and her mother weeping and blaming herself. 'If I hadn't been so horrible to Alwena she wouldn't have run away.'

The Child's parents had never been horrible to her. The Child's father had made her a garden of her very own, and even when she was very ill he would carry her to her garden and she would sit in her summerhouse and the birds would fly down to her shoulder and her pet fieldmice and hedgehogs would creep out to play round her feet. When her pets died, the gardener would dig a grave and bury them, and a pet-sized gravestone would be erected in their memory.

That's what the article in *Ceredigion* had said.

It was amazing to read about a Child who sounded just like *her*. 'Suffered ill-health throughout her childhood,' said the article, but it hadn't said what the illness was, or what had become of her. It did not even give her Christian name; she was simply described as the daughter of Sir Edward Jones-Mortimer, the man Alwena had heard T. J. speak of, who had bankrupted himself rebuilding Plas Idaleg after the great fire of 1807.

Alwena forgot about wanting to weep. The magnificent feeling of satisfaction she had experienced on reading these two or three lines about the Child returned to her. It did not matter how much her parents whispered about the Child now, she had begun to unravel the mystery for herself.

The next thing was to find the Child's Garden, which looked like being much more difficult.

The article had spoken of the Ladies' Walk with its Delightful Ambience, Lady Felicity's Garden with its Secluded Grotto, the Riverside Path with its Awesome Cataracts, all leading to the Magical Discovery of the Pensile, or Child's Garden with its Most Wondrous Prospect of the Mountains. It made the grounds of Plas Idaleg sound like something out of the Arabian Nights. But when Alwena looked about her she could see nothing but forestry plantations and rhododendrons.

What I need is a map, thought Alwena. It was odd that the article hadn't included a map. When it was written, the gardens must have been so clearly laid out you didn't need one.

A Most Wondrous Prospect of the Mountains. That must mean that the garden was high up in what now appeared to be the thickest, steepest part of the woods behind the house. Was that what Pensile meant?

She couldn't have been all that ill, thought Alwena, if they made her a garden at the top of a cliff.

'Alwena!' called her mother from the kitchen door, making her jump. 'Are you all right? You look as though you've been turned to stone. Have you seized up?'

'No, I'm fine, thank you.'

'You'll get cold, standing there.'

'I was just thinking.' Alwena stuck her stick into the ground and set off in the direction of the river. Bedwyr came out of the barn with a wisp of hay hanging from his mouth and followed her.

One good thing about her father being away at his meeting in Aberystwyth all day, he wasn't around to ask awkward questions about what she was doing and where she was going. Because if she *was* going to do some serious exploring to see if she could discover any of these lost gardens she would be forced to break the one rule her parents had made about her going for walks on her own, namely that she should not stray from the back or front drives, or the open parkland where she could be seen. She would need to strike into the woods, through the rhododendrons, the brambles and the bracken, where all sorts of obstacles and dangers might lie underfoot to trap her. If she fell, or if her joints suddenly failed her because she was exhausted, no-one would know where she was. She would have to be so careful.

The idea was frightening, but somehow exciting too. For the past two years, everyone had always known where she was, every single minute of the day.

I must find a map, she thought. Now would be a good chance to look for one in the library, while her father was out. Then tomorrow he would be so busy with these Sixth Formers, seeing that they got on with their work and didn't mess about or do any damage, the coast would be clear for her to start exploring properly.

She would have to wait until they had arrived and settled down to work. The thing would be to time it so that she could disappear before her mother tried to get her to go along when she took them their coffee.

Alwena made for the library, using the front entrance of Plas Idaleg so that her mother would not see her. It was essential that neither her mother nor her father should find out about her plan. If they did, they would be sure to stop her because it was dangerous. Worse, they might even offer to help.

Alwena did not want anyone to help her in her quest for the Child's Garden. It will be my secret, she thought. It will belong to me. Mum and Dad think the Child is their secret, but she's not. She's mine.

*   *   *

Gareth freewheeled down the hill and swerved over the ivy-covered bridge, the tyres of his mountain bike gripping the frosty road. His face burned and his eyes watered after his ride across the hills in the icy October air. He had not bothered to wear gloves and his hands were raw and stiff. By the row of grey cottages he braked to avoid a small group of elderly people who were crossing the road to board the Post Bus which would take them, very slowly, to Aberystwyth and back for their Saturday shopping. They turned to stare at Gareth as he pedalled past, watching carefully, he thought, to make sure they would know him again.

Before the right hand turn to Plas Idaleg, out of sight of the Lodge, he stopped and jumped off his bike, looking at his watch. At school yesterday afternoon Llŷr Hir had suddenly said to him, 'Are you still going tomorrow?'

'I thought I might as well. Gets me out of fitting kitchens with Dad.'

'I might come with you. It's not far on the bike.'

'What! I thought you were one of the pull-it-downers.'

'Mam says I ought to be interested,' said Llŷr. 'My Nain was a housemaid there, or something, before the war. I'll meet you by T. J.'s house, then, shall I? What time?'

Gareth had not wanted to get involved in arrangements of this sort. After a week spent poring over the Ordnance Survey map he wanted to do some exploring on the way to Plas Idaleg, and he did not want company. To his relief most of the group had been saying 'I might go to that Plas next Saturday,' in tones Gareth recognised as meaning 'I probably won't bother'. Gareth had not expected Llŷr's 'I might' to turn into 'I definitely will', but he minded him less than any of the others, especially Elin who had been driving him bats all week, wanting to talk about Their Relationship.

However he still did not want to be tied down to a rendezvous with Llŷr, so he said, 'See you about ten, then? But if I'm not there, don't wait, and if you're not there I won't wait either, okay?'

'Okay.' Llŷr had not really been listening. He won't turn up, thought Gareth.

It was now half-past nine. Gareth looked quickly back up the road to check that Llŷr was not about to appear, jumped on his bike and pedalled off, pushing hard on the pedals to build up speed for the steep gradient out of the village.

63

According to the map, the road leading east out of the village formed the northern boundary of the Plas Idaleg estate. He was pleased to see evidence for this in the remains of a high stone wall which ran alongside the right hand verge, very overgrown with moss and ivy and frequently buried in bracken. On the other side of the wall nothing could be seen but dense woodland which must be the same woods that rose up behind Plas Idaleg when you were looking at it from the front.

The road was narrow, twisty and hilly. It seemed to go on form miles, far longer than it looked on the map. Gareth stopped for a minute, wanting to check the map which he was carrying in his rucksack alongside his sandwiches and cans of lager. A man on a tractor drove by, lifting a hand in greeting and looking interestedly at Gareth as he passed.

It was too risky to get out the map. It was the actual map he had borrowed, not the copy he had intended to make. There was only one place in Abercoed where you could photocopy maps, at the back of the video shop, and the girl who worked there was Menna Williams, who had been Gareth's girlfriend for a while at school. She had left, to his relief, last year after GCSE. If he took something along to her for photocopying, she would think it was because he still fancied her. And sure as fate Elin would find out and he would be in trouble with her again as well.

Menna worked most Saturdays so she must have time off in the week sometimes. It was a nuisance, but he would just have to watch his opportunity for visiting the video shop when she was not there.

The stone wall was very tumbledown in places but it didn't seem to have any openings or entrances. Trees soared above him on both sides of the road now, the Sitka spruce plantation bare of undergrowth on his left and a dense mix of fir trees, rowans, oaks and beeches in every shade of green and brown behind the wall on his right. Gareth began to believe he was lost. This could not be the same road as the one on the map. He'd better turn back, it was ten to ten already.

Wait a moment, there was a building ahead. A building with a castellated tower built, it must be, from the same stone as the Plas. It was a church. Gareth dismounted from his bike and looked over a low wall into a grassy churchyard full of tombstones. A very dirty old grey Renault was parked by the wooden gate. Gareth groaned. It was T. J.'s car.

Gareth turned his bike round, jumped on and cycled hard back up the road, not stopping until he was out of sight of the church. There was a passing space on the left, scooped out of a breach in the wall, and he braked thankfully into it to get his breath. As he leaned, panting, on his bike he noticed a gate, set at an angle to the road and almost hidden in nettles so that it could not be seen when you were approaching from the other direction.

It was not a tidy Forestry Commission gate with a fire warning attached to it. It was a rusty, broken iron gate through which could be seen a soggy-looking track overgrown with nettles and willowherb and sloe bushes laden with dark blue fruit. Within a few yards the track was swallowed up by rhododendron-infested woodland. There were no recent tractor tyre marks, nor any flattened semi-circles of nettles which would show that the gate had been opened recently.

Anxious not to encounter T. J. Gareth climbed over the gate and hauled his bike over after him. He plunged along the track until he was out of sight of the road. The frost had not penetrated here and his feet slipped in the soggy ground. Soon his trainers and the legs of his jeans were splashed with mud. He struggled on, hauling his bicycle with him, using it as a shield to thrust his way through the brambles.

Presently he paused, furious with himself for having been such a fool as to venture so far from the main road. At this rate he would not reach the Plas before lunchtime, and furthermore would arrive covered with mud from head to foot. The sensible thing would be to turn back right now.

Except that the track might be a short-cut to the house, down through these woods. He'd just carry on a bit further and see.

The path zig-zagged steeply through the undergrowth and the trees which clung to the side of the hill. He must have been right about the gate, this could not be Forestry Commission land, there were too many different kinds of trees, mostly with much thicker trunks than the Sitkas, as though they were much older.

After a few hundred yards the path opened out onto a clearing where a few trees had been felled, although not recently judging by the lichen and fungi which grew all over the stumps. The mud gave way to a rather springy, dry carpet of fallen leaves and pine needles with an earthy, resinous scent. Gareth propped his bike and himself against a tree trunk. He shook off his rucksack, took out a can of lager and drank thankfully.

Half past ten. Llŷr would certainly have arrived at the Plas by now, and would have been set to work by Roscoe Morgan. All on his own with Roscoe Morgan, at least until T. J. arrived. No doubt Roscoe Morgan would be making remarks about people who were so keen to help one week and didn't bother to turn up the next. Gareth pictured himself staggering up the steps of Plas Idaleg, covered with mud, proving his determination to make it come hell or high water. The expression on Roscoe Morgan's face at the sight of him would be something not to be missed. Grinning in anticipation, Gareth finished his lager and stood up. He put the empty can back in his rucksack. At least he could make sure Roscoe Morgan couldn't get him for dropping litter.

He looked around the clearing. There seemed to be no way out. Behind him the land rose steeply in what must be the direction of the road—the way he had just come, although the track was invisible from where he stood. In front of him the clearing seemed to end abruptly, like the edge of a cliff. He could make out the remains of a wooden fence, and in the distance he could hear the sound of rushing water.

It had to be the same river that ran through the park surrounding the Plas. Holding onto the trunk of a birch sapling Gareth leaned cautiously over the fence. He was looking down what appeared to be a cliff face; rocks jutted out and ferns and stunted birch trees grew out of crannies. At the bottom he could see a vast thicket of rhododendron bushes, but no water and no sign of the lower levels of any path. Fall into that little lot and he'd be well and truly done for.

He'd have to go back the way he came. Hesitating, he looked across the clearing to where the ground rose again. More rocks and bracken and birch saplings and other plants Gareth could not name, but it looked navigable. Leaving his bike where he had propped it, but putting on his rucksack, Gareth began to scramble up the rocks, expecting to come across the estate wall within a few yards.

But the ground rose, and rose. Gareth climbed, using the rocks and vegetation as hand and footholds. Strange, aromatic scents rubbed off on his hands from the plants. There seemed to be an incredible variety of them, in all shades of green even at this time of year, and quite different from the bracken and stuff growing everywhere else.

This is ridiculous, he thought. I'm even more lost than I was before. He hauled himself onto an outcrop of rock to rest, and looked down. He could still just about make out his bike propped against its tree.

He had climbed high, but still the trees towered above him. They were pine trees, but their trunks were enormous. Their roots curled out of the earth, clutching the hillside like great swollen fingers.

The ground was levelling out again at last. If he went a bit further he would surely be able to look down on the Plas.

Ten more minutes, then he would turn back.

Odd how different the plants were up here. Even the rocks looked different, draped with bright green moss. It was very high up. But then there were rhododendrons again, thicker than ever. Gareth groaned with frustration and swiped at the nearest bush. It gave under his hand and he looked beyond to a rocky clearing decked with bracken and old heather and fringed with orange-berried rowan trees. The sun flashed on a small stream which tumbled between the rocks and out of sight behind what looked like the ivy-covered remains of a stone wall.

Gareth scrambled cautiously towards where the stream disappeared. There seemed to be some sort of square pillar, or column, a bit lower down. He could just see its pointed top. He stood up and looked around to try and get his bearings.

Then he saw the view.

Gareth had lived all his life in the hills of Cardiganshire. He was used to views. But this was something else.

The distances were hazy, immense, shimmering blue in the morning light. Gareth clutched at a branch to steady himself. It was as though he had been transported into one of those enormous paintings in the National Museum in Cardiff, with forests and lakes and mountains and gods and goddesses pouring wine out of golden pitchers.

As he gazed, the air was split by a clap of sound that seemed to lift his whole body from the earth.

Bloody jets! Gareth clapped his hands over his ears. Then because he quite enjoyed watching a jet roar across the sky he strained back to see if he could spot it.

The sky was quite clear. The jet must have been flying so low that the trees obscured it. Plas Idaleg was probably a navigation point. Gareth thought with satisfaction of Roscoe Morgan having to clap his hands over his ears on a regular basis.

Odd how it had disappeared so quickly. You could usually hear them for ages. Perhaps the woods absorbed the sound, or something—

'Hell *fire*! That was close!' Gareth ducked as the dreadful sound shrieked out again. It was as though something was tearing the rocks out of the earth. The rhododendrons shook. They carried on shaking, and a large grey donkey came struggling through the gap.

Chapter Five

'I'm sorry I'm late,' said Gareth.

He stood in the doorway of the Octagon Library, trying to keep his muddy trainers out of sight. T. J. was sitting at a large trestle table placed directly under the lantern window to get the best of the light. On the table was yet another pile of books with flaking brown covers. T. J. was checking each one against a list, sucking on his unlit pipe as he worked. Llŷr, looking fed up, was dusting the volumes of an old encyclopaedia and putting them on a shelf. Gareth looked warily for Roscoe Morgan, but he was not in the room.

Llŷr saw Gareth first.

'What time do you call *this*?'

'I must have taken a wrong turning,' said Gareth. 'I got lost.'

'Did you fall into a bog as well?'

'Sort of.' Gareth was about to launch into the story he had thought up about a tractor and trailer driving him into a ditch, then caught T. J.'s eye and changed his mind.

'Leave it dry, it'll soon brush off,' said T. J. 'We'll be stopping for a break in a minute. Did you bring sandwiches?'

'Yes.' Gareth slid his rucksack to the ground, thankful that he had not left it in the woods with his bicycle. He grinned at Llŷr, wondering how to rope him in to help retrieve the bike at the end of the afternoon.

Llŷr made a rude gesture and slammed the pages of the book he was dusting together. A cloud of dust flew up and they all coughed.

'Welcome to the coal-face,' said Llŷr. 'What was that disease they used to get in the lead mines, T. J.? I bet you could get it just as easy working in a library.'

'It'll take more than a few mornings humping books to give you pneumoconiosis, Llŷr, even here,' said T. J. He began to cough again and took out a handkerchief to wipe his watering eyes. 'Now then, Gareth, I'm putting you in charge of journals. They hold the dust even more than books, so we'd better not let Llŷr get near them.'

Llŷr banged his chest and made exaggerated choking noises, then stopped suddenly. Roscoe Morgan came into the room, carrying a tray. He looked disgruntled and he frowned even harder when he saw Gareth.

'I'm sorry I'm late,' said Gareth again, moving behind the trestle table to hide the state of his jeans.

Roscoe Morgan put the tray on the table. On it was a large vacuum flask, three mugs and a plate of digestive biscuits. 'You've missed your coffee, then,' he said. 'We'd given you up. I told my wife to put only three mugs.'

'That's all right,' said Gareth. 'I've got a drink with me.' He nearly said 'a beer' but thought better of it.

'He can use the top of my flask,' said Llŷr helpfully.

'There won't be enough coffee,' said Gareth. 'It doesn't matter. It's my fault for being late.' Creep, he told himself.

'Gareth missed the turning,' T. J. told Roscoe Morgan. 'He must have got onto the Devil's Bridge road by mistake. It's easily done, when you come free-wheeling down that old hill.'

'You cycled from Abercoed!' Roscoe Morgan stared at Gareth as though noticing him for the first time. 'You could probably do with some coffee,' he added grudgingly. 'You must be cold.'

'It's only nine miles,' said Gareth.

'I told you he was keen,' said T. J. 'You're very taken with Plas Idaleg, aren't you, Gareth?'

'It's all right,' mumbled Gareth. He nodded his thanks as Roscoe Morgan handed him the cap of Llŷr's flask filled with coffee. 'It's very big,' he said, trying again.

'They weren't afraid to think big two hundred years ago,' said Roscoe Morgan. 'They had the courage to be idealistic. Dream dreams. Think big. Not like now, in this claustrophobic semi-detached twentieth century.'

The passion in his voice embarrassed the two boys. What a nutcase, thought Gareth. He looked around the eight-sided room with its rising tide of books. Why do they all have to be old books? he thought. Why can't they have new ones? It'll be a right mausoleum by the time they're finished.

'But you're thinking quite big now, aren't you?' Llŷr was saying. 'I mean, this Lottery application is for millions, isn't it?' The interest in his voice irritated Gareth. Get off my patch, he told Llŷr silently.

'It's a great opportunity,' said Roscoe Morgan. 'We mustn't be afraid of it.' He began to talk of the plans to renovate Plas Idaleg, to restore its gardens and re-plant its famous woods. Gareth could not understand why it all sounded so depressing.

'It might be a good thing,' conceded Llŷr, when Roscoe Morgan paused to take a swallow of coffee. 'Especially when you start getting students and that. It might liven the place up a bit. I mean, there's not a lot going for people round here, is there?'

Roscoe Morgan seemed not to know whether he agreed with this or not. He seemed confused by the mention of students, as though he had forgotten what Plas Idaleg was being renovated for. He did not reply to Llŷr's remark. He turned to T. J. as though looking for help.

To break the silence, Gareth said, 'My Dad says there's an old story about this house. Something about a Child. In the olden days. He said you'd know about it.'

'The Child!' said Roscoe Morgan. 'Who told you about that?'

'I dunno,' said Gareth. 'It was just something my Dad said.'

And all those slamming doors, and barking dogs, and heads that bobbed out of sight.

It had happened again that morning. As he had pushed and slid through the undergrowth after that donkey, steeper and steeper downhill, he had felt sure he was being observed. Then the brambles had cleared abruptly and he had found himself on a rough track which opened out onto the Plas Idaleg park. As he set off towards it he could still feel the eyes of the watcher at his back.

First inside the house, he thought, and now outside. It can't be kids from the village, there's nobody there under seventy. Anyway, if it was kids I would have heard them.

'Your Dad must be thinking of Ann Jones-Mortimer,' said T. J., taking his pipe out of his mouth and starting to scrape out the bowl with a matchstick. He was watching Roscoe Morgan as he spoke. Let me tell the story, his look said.

*   *   *

No!

Alwena had to stop herself from crying aloud. It was not right that these boys, these strangers, should know about the Child when she was not allowed to. She bit her knuckles furiously and wedged herself more firmly behind the open library door, listening as hard as she could.

She had only just got there in time, lurking out of sight until the Boy had disappeared into the house and her father had crossed the yard with the tray of coffee. Then she stumbled across the grass with the aid of her stick and climbed the steps into the house, forcing herself to hurry. Pain stabbed in her knees and she longed to sit down, but there was nowhere to sit but the floor, and nowhere to conceal herself except behind the library door.

She was still furious with the boy Gareth. He had staggered out of the wood and thrown his arms round Bedwyr's neck to stop himself falling over. He had no business to be in the woods. He was trespassing. Her father was right, he was a vandal, up to no good. She must not let him out of her sight.

And now T. J. was going to tell him about the Child, and her father was doing nothing to stop him.

*   *   *

'She was a bit of a prodigy,' said T. J. 'She had all the accomplishments that young girls were supposed to have in those days, playing the piano, drawing, sewing and so forth.'

Boring, thought Gareth. Wouldn't you guess?

'But more than that, she loved the gardens and the woods. She was an expert little botanist, collected specimens, kept notebooks which she illustrated herself—they would be very valuable if they still existed. Her father was always inviting eminent botanists and scientists and suchlike to Plas Idaleg to talk about all his reforming ideas and they all went mad over his daughter, about how intelligent she was and what a pity she was a girl and so couldn't study the sciences at university.'

Roscoe Morgan put down his coffee mug with a bang which was clearly meant to indicate that they had spent enough time talking and should get on with some work. Gareth and Llŷr fidgeted.

'Her father thought the world of her,' continued T. J., serenely cleaning his pipe. 'He built a garden for her, up on the rocks. He built a summer house and imported all sorts of rare alpine plants. She used to go there all the time, even after she was ill. They built a special chair for her, to carry her up. You know, she never stopped reading about plants and animals, and writing about them and drawing them, no matter how poorly she was.' T. J. put his cleaned pipe back into his mouth. 'People used to come from all over to see the garden,' he continued. 'The view was famous. It's all overgrown now, I daresay. You'd never find it.'

That's where I was this morning, thought Gareth, his boredom evaporating. I did find it. I must've done. That view.

He tried to keep his face impassive. Everybody knew that T. J. could read minds.

'What happened?' asked Llŷr.

'Well, you know, it all gets a bit vague,' said T. J. 'Especially after the fire. Sir Edward went bankrupt and they moved down south somewhere for a few years. They say little Ann was devastated. She lived for the time when they could come back to Plas Idaleg.'

'And did they?'

'People used to say they never knew whether the Jones-Mortimers were in residence or not. They used to flit back and forth—I suppose that's how the story started.'

'It's all nonsense,' interrupted Roscoe Morgan. 'I'm

76

surprised at you, T. J.' He began to drag boxes of books across the floor with furious energy.

'Oh come on, T. J.,' said Llŷr. 'Don't tell us she haunts the place. The ghost of Plas Idaleg!'

T. J.'s eyes twinkled. 'People were very superstitious in those days,' he said. 'I'm sure there's nothing in it. What's the matter, Gareth? You don't believe in ghosts, do you?'

'No!' said Gareth.

As he spoke an icy draught cut across the room and the door of the library swung shut with a heavy thud. After a moment, Llŷr and T. J. began to laugh. Gareth's stomach returned to its normal position. He tried to join in the laughter but was arrested by the sight of Roscoe Morgan's face. It was white.

*   *   *

'Alwena, where on earth have you been?' asked her mother, looking up from a batch of photographic proofs as Alwena crept into the kitchen. 'What's the matter?'

'I don't feel very well,' quavered Alwena. 'I want to sit down.'

'Did those big boys frighten you, then,' teased her mother, laughing. Then she stopped, and a look of concern came over her face. 'You are stiff, aren't you? You've been out for ages, you must have overdone it. Come and sit in your wheelchair, and I'll run you a bath. Would you like a hot drink?' Alwena nodded. Her mother helped her into her chair and pushed it over by the kitchen range.

Ann Jones-Mortimer.

77

She knew the Child's name at last.

She was probably horrible, thought Alwena, half asleep. Her and her botany. Horrible clever-clogs.

Alwena was furious that she had lived at Plas Idaleg all this time without Ann Jones-Mortimer having appeared out of the shrubbery to introduce herself. If she haunted the place, she should have noticed Alwena. It would only have been polite.

It spoiled things, knowing the Child's name. She was now not a Child, but a person. Ann Jones-Mortimer. Upper class and posh, bound to be, her father being a Sir and all that. She'd speak English all the time. Too grand to mix with the local children, or anyone who lived at Plas Idaleg after her.

I bet she wasn't as ill as I am, thought Alwena. I bet her father didn't look after her as well as Dad looks after me. She probably had hundreds of servants to do all the work. I bet she wasn't all that clever really, they just thought she was because she was interested in science. I bet that was unusual for a girl in the olden days.

It was unusual enough even now. Alwena thought physics and chemistry and biology were pretty boring, herself, and she didn't care two hoots about going to University.

All the same, it was annoying to hear that this Ann Jones-Mortimer had had ambitions despite being ill. As well as being ill. As though the illness was only secondary.

She can't have been all that ill, Alwena repeated to herself. Real illness, illness like hers which still might leave her permanently disabled, didn't leave time for anything else. She'd only recently started doing lessons again and they were tiring enough.

Besides, it depended on the ambition. You could perhaps be a scientist in a wheelchair, like that man in Cambridge David had told her about, but the only thing Alwena had ever wanted to be was a riding instructress and she'd stopped thinking about *that* years ago. Because of course it was quite impossible now.

Her illness had put an end to all her old ambitions, all her old life.

But there had been no Plas Idaleg in her old life. No great house, no forest, no mountains, no hidden gardens. No Child.

I must find the garden, thought Alwena. I'll restore it. That will be my ambition. I won't tell anyone, though, not even Dad. Then when I find it, it will be my garden, and I'll be allowed to stay there, and look after it forever and ever. And if Ann What's-her-name is still haunting it she'll just have to get used to me.

Her thoughts became more jumbled. She dozed off. She was woken by her mother gently laying a hand on her forehead.

'I've run the bath. There's just time before lunch, if we're quick.'

Alwena sat up with a jerk. She yawned.

'Perhaps you'd better rest in bed for a while this afternoon,' said her mother. 'Just to be on the safe side.'

'All right,' agreed Alwena, thinking of the *Ceredigion* article in her drawer. It would be a good chance to read it again, really study it this time. If she was going to find the garden she had better get a move on. Now that T. J.

was telling everyone about it the whole world would soon be crashing about in the woods searching for the old paths and walks. In fact, remembering that boy with the long hair, that Gareth, hanging on to Bedwyr for dear life as he emerged from the undergrowth that very morning, it looked as though at least one person had started already.

Chapter Six

'That's better,' said Alwena's father, taking a deep, contented breath and looking round at the autumn landscape. 'Woods, birds, sheep and peace.'

Alwena was sitting in the saddle on Bedwyr's back, her feet dangling in the stirrups, the reins hooked loosely through her bent fingers. Her father held a leading rein clipped to Bedwyr's bit as they pottered across the turf towards the river. The way Bedwyr's ears drooped told her exactly what he felt about this.

'It's good to have the place to ourselves, isn't it,' said her father. 'I wish we could do this more often, go for walks like this, just you and me.'

It was Sunday afternoon and even T. J. had gone home after another morning's cataloguing, coughing hard to clear the dust from his lungs.

Alwena said nothing. How could her father believe that they had, or had ever had, the place to themselves when it was clearly still inhabited by the Child and *her* father?

When she did not speak Alwena's father stopped, and

turned to her with a questioning look. 'Alwena? Are you tired? Shall we go back?'

'No, no, I'm fine.'

After a moment he said, 'You are happy, Alwena, aren't you? Now you're getting better?'

'Yes, of course I am.'

'Your mother thinks you might be lonely.'

'I'm not a bit lonely, Daddy. I love being here with you and Mum, and T. J. and Bedwyr and Olwen. Especially when it's all quiet and empty, like today.' She knew this was what he wanted her to say.

Besides, it was true. She had liked it best when they had Plas Idaleg to themselves. But they did not have it to themselves any more. They had to share it with Ann Jones-Mortimer and her father. Alwena felt pushed out by Ann Jones-Mortimer. She was cleverer, for one thing. All those accomplishments. She had had a more serious illness too, and a nobler nature, not letting her illness get in the way of her studies.

Alwena supposed she should be grateful that her parents had not rammed this paragon of a Child down her throat, but had tried to avoid mentioning her at all. She thought she understood why, now.

They continued to walk along the river bank, listening to the sound of the fast-running water. Bedwyr plodded along grudgingly, his flat back swaying as he walked. Alwena held onto the pommel of the saddle to balance herself. He did not feel in the least like a pony to ride.

Ahead of them stood the moss-covered stone walls of the old kitchen garden. The branches of a few ancient apple trees could be seen above a sea of stinging nettles.

'When we get the Lottery money,' said Alwena's father, 'the first thing I want to tackle is the vegetable garden. We could be completely self-sufficient in fruit and vegetables if we went about it in the right way. Two hundred years ago it would have been taken for granted.'

'For the Centre, you mean?'

'I keep telling the Trustees, it's a fantastic opportunity to preserve the garden and grow food for the Centre.'

'I wish we could have horses in the stables again,' said Alwena. 'And carriages instead of cars.'

'So do I,' said her father. 'It would be more in keeping with the spirit of the place.'

They both knew that in the new plans for Plas Idaleg the stables were to be converted into visitor accommodation and laboratories.

'I worry that we're compromising too much,' said her father. 'It's all money these days, that's the trouble. Nothing can exist for its own sake, simply because it's noble and beautiful. It has to make money. I seem to do nothing but produce business plans. Sir Edward Jones-Mortimer would have despised the very idea of a business plan. No doubt our young Sixth Former friends would disapprove of him for putting everything he had into making something beautiful. They forget he was trying to improve the economy of the area as well. Planting trees, bringing in new farming methods. They call it job creation these days and you can get EEC grants for it—'

Alwena listened to her father rambling on. He seemed no longer to be addressing her but some imaginary committee, banging his fists together to emphasise a point, and jerking the leading rein so that Bedwyr grunted and stopped dead. Alwena flapped her legs weakly against his sides to urge him on but he paid no attention.

'He even set up his own printing press,' said her father, apparently not noticing that they had come to a halt. 'Two hundred years ago. No computers then.'

Alwena thought, no, and I bet Ann Jones-Mortimer wouldn't have known how to work one, even if there had been. I'd have had to show her how to do it.

Alwena felt encouraged by this realisation. 'I don't mind computers,' she told her father.

'Yes, your mother tells me you've left her a long way behind on the computer front.' He sighed. 'That's one of the reasons she's anxious for you to go back to school.'

When Alwena did not reply he said, 'Perhaps we should be looking at some private tuition for you. Someone from the Maths department, say? How would you feel about that?'

Ann Jones-Mortimer would have had tutors, thought Alwena. She wouldn't have gone to school at all.

A picture flashed into her mind of all the archaeologists and architects and other clever people who would be coming to Plas Idaleg when the Study Centre opened. They would be amazed by the Warden's brilliant daughter. Her father would like that.

The truth was, though, she was not brilliant. Computers weren't a subject in themselves, like Maths. They were just machines. Her mother and father didn't understand that. They thought that it took great intelligence to understand computers. A tutor from the Maths department would not be so easily misled.

Still, it might be better than going back to school.

Alwena envisaged herself back at school, surrounded by large noisy people like that Gareth and his friends. The memory of their loud conversation and raucous jokes and giggles came back to her, flooding her brain with a cacophony of voices. She could no more talk like that than fly to the moon.

You know what I *mean*, she said silently to Ann Jones-Mortimer.

'I wouldn't mind a tutor,' she said aloud to her father.

*   *   *

'What's he doing here again?' demanded Alwena indignantly, two days later. She grabbed a barking Olwen and ducked out of sight below the conservatory window sill as Gareth freewheeled down the drive to Plas Idaleg and jumped off at the foot of the steps to the front entrance.

Pulling Olwen after her Alwena went in search of her father, finding him in the little ante-room to the library which served as his office.

'That Gareth is here again,' she reported breathlessly. 'It's *Tuesday*.'

'Oh yes,' said her father, looking up from the morning's letters and pulling a face. 'Friend Gareth. It's half term. He wants to draw the house. He's doing Art for his A Levels or something.'

I bet T. J. fixed this up, thought Alwena. He pushed Dad into it. Sometimes she wondered whose side T. J. was really on.

She listened by the library door to make sure Gareth

84

had not entered the house, then made for the back staircase with Olwen trotting at her heels. She hauled herself to the top and limped along the long gallery to her favourite of the front-facing rooms, the one she would have chosen for herself given the opportunity. It was a corner room with tall, narrow sash windows divided by an old, speckled looking-glass. Pretty pointed arches made of carved white plaster, like wedding cake icing, decorated the faded blue walls. There were fewer holes in the wall and the floor than in the rest of the house, and the late October sun shining through the windows made it feel as warm as the conservatory.

Perhaps it was Her room, thought Alwena. Ann Jones-Mortimer's room. Well, it's mine now.

She pressed her face against one of the sash windows, then stepped back quickly as she saw Gareth walk away from the house. Holding Olwen, Alwena watched as he slipped off his rucksack and opened it. He took out quite a large, flat sketchbook and turned over the pages, looking at the house as he did so. He looked around, then went and sat on a nearby rock which stuck out of the turf. After a while he took out a pencil and began to chew it.

Alwena thought, he's going to be there all *day*.

It wasn't fair. She wouldn't be able to do any proper exploring if that boy was going to keep popping up all over the place.

Without her stick Alwena could not stand for very long before her legs and back began to ache and her balance began to go. There was no furniture in the room so she hobbled to the door and held on to it. Olwen ran back to the window and jumped her front paws onto the sill. She looked out with a bark, her short whip of a tail quivering.

'Olwen! Come here! Be quiet!'

Olwen got down with a sigh, and came over to Alwena with a reproachful look on her long, ugly bull terrier's face.

'I know we ought to watch him,' Alwena told her. 'But he mustn't see us.'

She could still just see him from where she stood. The sun shone brightly on his fair hair, it was impossible not to see him. His head was bent over his drawing pad now. After a moment or two he glanced up, tossing his hair back as he did so. Why didn't he get it *cut*? thought Alwena, echoing her father's continual complaint.

Her father seemed to take the boy Gareth's long hair very personally.

'You're a fine one to talk,' her mother had retorted at one point. 'When I first met you your hair was much longer than that. And it wasn't as clean either.'

Her father with long hair? It was impossible to imagine.

'Well, I can't stand here all day watching somebody's hair,' said Alwena aloud, as though it was all the boy's fault.

As she stumped downstairs she could hear her mother calling her from the library.

'We can't do lessons today!'

'Why not?' said her mother, pulling out her chair for her.

'It's half term! It's half term, isn't it, Dad!'

86

Her father looked out of his office. 'It is, as a matter of fact. The boy's here,' he said to Alwena's mother. 'In the park. Drawing.'

'Ah. I see.' Alwena's mother smiled drily. 'Very well. But you'd better have a holiday task. A project. What about a bit of botany? I know it's the wrong time of year, but there are still a lot of plants about. Mushrooms too.'

Alwena pouted. 'It's cold,' she said. And besides, I'm not like your precious Child, she thought. I'm not interested in science. Then it occurred to her that searching for plants would be a useful cover for some exploring.

'All right,' she said. 'But not today. Not while he's here. Can't I do a reading project as well?'

She knew this would please her mother, who was always reading and who had been disappointed when Alwena had shown so little inclination to read while she was ill.

'You bought me all those paperbacks and I haven't read half of them.'

'Well! You must be getting better!' She looked as if she were about to say, 'Soon have you back at school!' but changed her mind.

Alwena thought, I wonder if Dad's mentioned the Maths tutor yet.

*   *   *

Gareth shifted about on his uncomfortable rock seat, trying to remember what Claire Davies, his Art teacher at school, had taught him about perspective. He'd

87

forgotten how much harder it was to draw from life, with a pencil, rather than from his head, with a mouse on a computer screen.

Besides, Plas Idaleg was so elaborate. Nothing more different from a tower block could be imagined. It was all arches, and turrets, and battlements. Even the campanile, though plainer than the rest of the house, had elaborate brickwork which was amazingly difficult to draw.

The truth was, it was quite an ugly house, for all its grandeur. A magnificent hotchpotch, he thought, trying the phrase out for possible use in his History paper.

What the hell was a house like this doing in the middle of the Welsh mountains anyway? It ought to be in Italy or France, or somewhere sinister like Turkey or Bulgaria. Transylvania. The Carpathians. Gareth rolled the names on his tongue, feeling gloriously far from home.

He had borrowed his father's bicycle to come to Plas Idaleg today, without telling him. His own bike was still where he had left it somewhere up in that wood, and he had no idea how he was going to retrieve it. He'd got himself home last Saturday by walking as far as Llŷr's parents' farm, and getting a lift with Llŷr and his elder brother when they set off to Lampeter for their Saturday night drink.

He'd been made to sit down to wait by a Rayburn in a black-painted inglenook, facing a sharp-eyed crone who had turned out to be Llŷr's Nain, the one who had once worked as a housemaid at Plas Idaleg.

'Tell him about Plas Idaleg,' Llŷr had shouted in her ear. 'Plas Idaleg! That's where we've been today!'

'It was a very fine place,' the old woman had replied, after thinking for a long time. 'The old gentleman was always very fair.'

'What about the ghost?' shouted Llŷr.

'Always plenty of food at Plas Idaleg. And fires, too.'

'The ghost!'

She had shaken her head, her face creased with laughter. 'No no, no ghost.'

Gareth had felt relieved and disappointed at the same time.

In the park at Plas Idaleg he persevered with his drawing. He wanted to draw the house from every angle, from a distance and in close-up. He needed a good stack of work to show Claire Davies after half term. She had given him a tremendous ticking-off for idleness a week or two ago and he didn't want her to repeat it at the parents' evening which was scheduled for next week. His mother would be furious with him for wasting his opportunities and his father would be furious with him for wasting his time at school when he could be apprenticing himself as a plumber. There would be no peace for months.

Peace enough here, all right. He'd better make the most of it. Better out in the open than in the house with that twitchy Roscoe Morgan on the prowl all the time. Gareth badly wanted to explore the house but fat chance there would be of that with him about.

Roscoe Morgan didn't like strangers, it was obvious. He wanted to keep the place to himself. Gareth didn't blame him, really. You could tell it had been T. J.'s idea to bring the A Level History group to the house. T. J.

was like that. He decided you ought to do something, and whatever *you* felt about the idea you found yourself doing it. As though he felt the need to give the world a push now and again, to keep it turning.

These thoughts drifted through Gareth's mind as he sketched. Gradually his concentration focused and he began to draw in more detail. After a while he moved closer to the house to draw the doors and the arched windows, then backed away in the direction of the river to draw the south facing wall of the house. A conservatory covered with scarlet virginia creeper ran along the ground floor. The sunlight flashed on the windows. Here and there the glass had gone, leaving black squares like lost teeth.

No bobbing heads or barking dogs today. The house seemed deserted, except for the grey donkey which grazed nearby.

After a while he began to feel cold and stiff. Looking at his watch he saw that it was after three. Well, he'd done plenty of work. He stood up, stretched, and walked to the campanile where he had left the bike propped up against the wall with his rucksack.

The front door of the Plas was shut. Gareth wondered whether he ought to seek out Roscoe Morgan to let him know he was leaving, but it seemed easier not to. Besides if he left now, there would be time before it got dark to cycle round that back road to see if he could find his way into the woods where he had left his own bike. If he could rescue it he could at least get it over to Llŷr's, where it could be left for the time being. Gareth looked at his watch again and stuffed his last sandwich into his mouth. Then with a last look at the house he hoisted on his rucksack, mounted his bike and pedalled away.

*   *   *

After lunch Alwena went back to her observation point in the blue room. Gareth was still there, drawing away. Down by the river now. He wouldn't be able to see the back of the house at all.

Her father was in his little office next to the Octagon library. Her mother had driven to Aberystwyth for her Tuesday afternoon aerobics class at the Sports Centre. Alwena was supposed to be in the sitting room reading *The Mill on the Floss* but the presence of Gareth in the park made her feel restless.

He needs keeping an eye on, her father had said. He's not to be trusted.

What had he been doing with Bedwyr in the woods the other day, for example? He had no business being in the north drive at all, it was not a right of way and no one ever used it except a few farmers and forestry workers.

It wouldn't take ten minutes to go and have a look. If he had done any damage she would tell her father. She felt a rush of spiteful pleasure at the prospect of finding something to report.

She put on outdoor clothes and wellingtons, called Olwen and picked up her walking stick. The wing of the house where the Morgans lived could not be seen from the front, and by skirting the old stable block she could reach the north drive under the shelter of a straggle of hawthorn bushes.

According to the *Ceredigion* article you approached

the Child's Garden from the north drive by what it described as 'a most tortuous steep path'. But there was no clear indication as to where on the north drive the path started from, and she had been able to find no map to help her.

Not that he would have found the path, surely. Probably he'd just gone behind a bush to relieve himself. That still didn't explain what he was doing on the north drive in the first place.

It was quite easy to find the spot where he had burst out of the rhododendrons. Crushed leaves and broken branches still hung from the bushes, the fallen leaves were flattened and the bracken was trampled down. Olwen scrabbled in the undergrowth, snuffling excitedly.

Alwena stepped carefully, one foot after the other, onto the trampled bracken and behind the bush from which Gareth and Bedwyr had appeared so suddenly. She found herself looking up a steep, wooded hillside. Rhododendrons, bracken and brambles surged round the trunks of huge oak, beech and pine trees. Here and there cliffs of moss-covered rock broke through the undergrowth like a massive staircase.

Feeling dizzy, Alwena looked down at her feet again. Ahead of her she could make out a trail of trodden-down grass and bracken curving upwards through the bushes. She took an uncertain step forward, prodded with her stick, and stepped forward again.

It was not a path exactly, but someone had certainly been this way recently.

I'll just see how far it goes, thought Alwena. I won't go far from the drive. Just a few steps.

'Come on, Olwen!'

Olwen ran up to her with a bark.

'Let's follow the trail, Olwen, and see where it leads.'

Prod, step, prod. Olwen shot ahead of her, then ran back impatiently.

'You'll have to wait for me. You know I'm slow.'

The trail was still there. It was not too steep. She would just go a bit further. As long as she had Olwen with her she was safe.

It still wasn't too steep. Now the trail turned back on itself, and disappeared. No, no, there it was again—oh, *drat* these rhododendrons.

'Olwen! Wait! Come back!' She waited, but there was no response. She could hear panting and rustling noises ahead of her as Olwen scrambled diligently upwards. There was nothing for it but to follow. Her heart thumping with a mixture of excitement and fear, Alwena prodded after her dog. There was no doubt about it, this was a proper adventure. Her parents would be horrified if they could see her. The trail was getting steeper now. Prod, step, prod, catch at a tree trunk. *Don't look down.*

She rested on a rock to get her breath. How green the rocks were, with all the brilliant mosses. Some of the mosses were like miniature ferns, others like tresses of long green hair. Nearby she could hear the sound of splashing water. The wind sighed in the treetops, and autumn leaves fluttered by. It was very peaceful.

Just a bit farther, thought Alwena, biting her lip with determination as she pulled herself carefully to her feet with the aid of her stick and balanced herself on her feeble ankles.

There was a steep bit coming now. Perhaps she should not attempt it. Even as she was telling herself this she was prodding forwards, catching at a sapling to balance herself. Oh! She nearly slipped just then! Oh, her knees were aching.

She should not have started this. She should just have gone home and told her father. Whatever had possessed her to keep climbing onwards?

It must have been Gareth who had made this trail. He must have taken a short cut from the main road. Hadn't she overheard him saying something about getting lost?

Alwena clutched at her stick. She badly wanted to sit down again, but there was no convenient rock, the bracken was so wet and the brambles so thorny. Her jeans were soaking. She knew she must keep moving now; if her legs got cold she would get cramp and be unable to move. Nobody knew where she was. If she fell—if she slipped—where was Olwen?

'Olwen!' she cried. 'Olwen!'

Ahead of her the track turned on itself again in the lee of a rocky cliff. She struggled forward a few steps and leaned on it thankfully. Her heart was pounding now. Her fingers were shaking. She could not make them close around her stick, and had to fold her arms across her chest to retain her hold on it.

After a few moments her heartbeat slowed and she could hear the woodland sounds again. Far away she could hear the bleat of sheep and the cry of ravens but she could not hear Olwen.

'Olwen! Olwen!'

Far above her she heard the distant sound of a bark.

94

She looked up, peering uncertainly, not daring to step away from the rock face.

'Olwen, come down!'

She's got stuck, thought Alwena. She must be stuck. She can't get down. I'll have to get her down.

She held her stick as firmly as her shaking hands would allow, and stepped onto the trail again. Almost immediately she tripped, but before she could cry out she had saved herself. The ground rose steeply again, but the trail left by Gareth and now Olwen seemed to have exposed what looked like natural steps in the rock, and Alwena had actually fallen up the steps. Panting hard, she pushed herself up the steps on her bottom, one by one, careless of what this would do to her clothes. It surely couldn't be much further now. She must be quite near the estate boundary—there was a wall—

The steps ended. Alwena got slowly to her feet and looked around. She seemed to have arrived in a small clearing dotted with trees, very tall trees with huge trunks. A few felled, or fallen, trees lay on the ground, which was flat and brown with a thick mattress of fallen leaves.

In the middle of the trees, propped against one of the felled tree trunks, was a bicycle.

Alwena let out a helpless sob of relief at this evidence of human presence. She went up to the bike and touched the handlebar. It felt wet and clammy. The saddle was wet, too. Now that she was close to it she could see that the whole machine was filmed with moisture. It had evidently been lying there overnight or longer.

It must be Gareth's bike. This must be where he had come down from.

He won't come back for it today, thought Alwena. He's got another bike today. You can't ride two bikes at once.

So she was still alone, lost in this wood. She looked up in horror at the soaring trees. Oh, *where* was Olwen?

'Olwen!'

Again that distant bark.

'Olwen, I *can't* come after you any more.'

Alwena ached all over. All the strength had drained from her legs and hands.

'Olwen!'

If Olwen didn't come now she didn't know what she was going to do.

This time there was no answering bark.

Where could she have gone to? There seemed to be no way out of the clearing except for a steep, grass-filled track that led in quite the opposite direction from where Olwen seemed to be barking. If I go that way I must surely come to the main road, thought Alwena. It can't be far.

But she couldn't leave Olwen. She might really be trapped somewhere. Alwena took a deep, shivery breath, trying not to cry. She stood up again, clasped her stick and prodded to the edge of the clearing.

Yes, there was another track here, and what looked like more steps in the rock. More green plants here too, not just moss, but other plants that Alwena had never seen before. They crept out of crevices and grew in mats across the rock. Some carried small, faded flower-heads.

It was then she knew that she was climbing up to the Child's Garden.

Olwen must have found the Child's Garden, and she was waiting for Alwena to find it too.

I can't, thought Alwena. I can't go any further. Her ankles gave way and she sank onto one of the steps in the rock. Tears of exhaustion filled her eyes.

It was no good, she would have to turn back. Go up that green track to the road. The Child's Garden wouldn't go away. She knew where it was now. She would come back tomorrow. She'd get her father to bring her.

He wouldn't do it, though. Alwena knew he would not. He would be horrified—and very angry—if he knew she had done this dangerous climb without his knowledge. She would not be allowed out on her own for weeks. Anyway she didn't want him to know about the Child's Garden, him or anyone else just yet.

So it was now or never.

She gathered her strength, and reached for the next step in the rock.

It was very steep here, but there had definitely once been proper steps. Presently the ground levelled, and she found herself in another rhododendron thicket.

'Olwen!'

There was a bark, and Olwen rushed joyfully out of the bushes. She danced round Alwena, then ran away again. Alwena followed, hobbling through the rhododendrons.

The world spread out before her.

Alwena stood quite still. It was as though her heart had stopped. Trembling, she felt for a dry rock to sit on, under an ancient beech tree. Olwen flopped at her feet, panting happily.

Alwena leaned back against the tree and closed her eyes. When she opened them she was still in the same

97

place. A stream tumbling down the rocks, then forests and mountains and sky to eternity. The sun was dropping towards the horizon, lighting the whole landscape with long rays of bronze.

The Child's Garden. Ann Jones-Mortimer's garden. It was like a huge overgrown rockery suspended from the side of the world. Looking at the dense green carpet of conifer forest flooding across the hills below her was like looking at the earth from an aeroplane.

Vertigo hit Alwena with a swaying nausea. She shrank against the rock, catching Olwen by the collar.

Olwen whimpered in protest. Suddenly her body stiffened and she began to bark. She barked and barked, wriggling in Alwena's failing grasp.

Alwena could hear scrambling footsteps. Somebody else was coming into the garden.

Her insides turned liquid. It's her, she thought wildly. It's the Child. It's Ann Jones-Mortimer. She was here all the time.

A face peered round the rhododendron bushes.

Chapter Seven

'Ann?'

Gareth heard his voice croaking a long way away.

The Child gasped.

The Child had a skinny, triangular face with huge dark eyes and a thin black fringe. She was bent forwards in a strange, twisted crouch, her arms wrapped round a hysterically barking dog with an ugly brown and white face.

Gareth stared at the dog, disoriented. Ghosts didn't have dogs. Slowly his stomach resumed its usual position as he realised that the Child had a twentieth century haircut and was wearing a very twentieth century parka of jazzy pinks and blues.

The Child opened and shut her mouth several times. 'I'm not her,' she said at last. 'I'm myself.' She seemed upset. Her face was very dirty and streaked with tears. 'I'm not *her*,' she repeated, sniffing hard.

'Sorry,' said Gareth. He giggled weakly. 'I thought you must be.' He stood for a moment, feeling stupid. His rucksack dragged on his shoulders. He took it off and scrambled down the rocks to where he could see her properly yet be out of the dog's reach. The dog stopped barking. It cowered between the girl's legs, glaring at him and growling.

'It must have been you I saw in the house as well,' he said. 'Plas Idaleg.'

'I live at Plas Idaleg,' said the girl with another sniff.

Gareth sat down carefully on a mossy rock. 'We've been going there,' he said. 'Saturdays. In the library.'

'I know, I've seen you.'

'Is Roscoe Morgan your Dad then?'

She nodded.

Gareth felt disappointed. All that mystery, and it was just a schoolgirl.

'Your name isn't Ann then.' He tried to make a joke of it.

'My name's Alwena,' said the girl crossly. 'Ann lived two hundred years ago.'

'My Dad had heard an old story,' said Gareth. 'About this Child that haunted Plas Idaleg. And we kept on hearing funny noises in the house. And I thought I saw—so we thought—' God, it sounded stupid. 'It must have been you.'

She must have been hiding from us, he thought. She didn't want to be seen. Or, Roscoe Morgan didn't want us to see her. Was that why he was so twitchy all the time?

Didn't want his daughter mixing with riff-raff like us, thought Gareth. I bet that's what it was.

'She might still be here,' said Alwena unexpectedly. 'Ann. Just because I'm not her it doesn't mean she's not here anyway.'

'What?'

'Nothing.' Alwena bent over her dog so that she could not see his face.

'Llŷr Hir's Nain laughed when I asked her about the ghost. She used to work at the Plas, before the war.'

'She can't have. Nobody's lived there except us for fifty years.'

'It was before the war like I said. She's very old.'

Gareth settled down on his rock and turned his face towards the view. There was still a little warmth in the sun. 'It's good here,' he said. 'Sheltered. And the view. No wonder she used to come here all the time. I would've if it'd been my garden. Not very easy to get to though, is it? Why don't you get your Dad to clear the path a bit?'

How his own father would relish the challenge. There'd be steps and a handrail put in before you could say concrete mixer. He grinned and the girl gave him a suspicious look that reminded him of her father.

She said, 'I've never been here before today. I didn't think anybody else knew about it. How did you find out about it?'

Gareth said evasively, 'I saw an old map. When I was sorting these old magazines out. It had a lot of old paths on it. And there's supposed to be waterfalls and caves and things.'

The map still lay, uncopied, in his rucksack.

'But I found it by accident really.'

The girl said nothing.

'There's supposed to be a waterfall up here somewhere,' he said. 'I can hear it, can you? Perhaps it's below us down by that monument thing.'

She did not reply. She did not even look in the direction of the pillar. He felt she was waiting for him to leave. Oh well, he knew when he wasn't wanted.

'I'm sorry to disturb you,' he said politely, standing up. 'I'll be off out of your way.'

Still Alwena did not speak, but he was alarmed to see that her eyes were filling with tears. He realised that she had a sweaty, feverish look, red-faced and exhausted like someone at the end of a long race. He watched her, not knowing what to do.

'Are you all right?'

Alwena took a deep, sobbing breath. Then she whispered, 'I can't get down.'

'What? Oh, yeah, it's a steep old climb, isn't it?'

She took another deep breath. 'The thing is,' she said, 'I can't walk very well.'

She had released her hold on the dog, and now he noticed that her fingers did not unbend themselves as anyone else's might have.

'What's the matter, have you had a fall?'

She shook her head wearily. 'I've been ill.'

'How did you get up here then? Did you come on the donkey?'

'The donkey! No, of course not.'

'I just thought,' said Gareth. 'He was here, last time. That was how I found my way down. I followed him.'

'Bedwyr was *here*?'

'Yes. Er, look, you'd better stay here while I go and find your Dad.'

He couldn't just leave her. It would make him late, but there was nothing he could do about that now.

'No!'

'What's the matter?' he asked impatiently.

Alwena whispered, 'I don't want my Dad to know I've been up here.'

'He'll be mad, will he?'

Alwena shook her head vehemently. 'He worries all the time.'

Won't let her do anything, thought Gareth. Poor kid. He said, 'I don't know how you managed to get up here. If you've been ill, like.'

'I'm better some days than others,' said Alwena. 'I found the path, and it went on longer than I thought. And then Olwen ran off.'

Hearing her name, the dog barked.

'Got a horrible looking face, hasn't she?' said Gareth.

'She's a very nice dog,' said Alwena. 'She can't help what she looks like. She's a bull terrier. They're very loyal.'

'Not if they run off, they aren't.' Gareth sighed as his attempt at humour died on him. 'Look, what are we going to do? Shall I go and see if I can find the donkey? Has he got a saddle and bridle?'

'No, no—his tack's in the house.' She thought for a moment, then felt in her coat pocket and brought out a leather dog-lead. 'You could put this round his neck, p'raps,' she suggested. 'Olwen doesn't need it with me. Only when there's sheep.'

'Okay, I'll try,' said Gareth. 'But look, you know, if I can't catch him or something I'll have to tell your Mum and Dad.'

'It's just that—' Alwena looked at the ground. She seemed near to tears once more. 'All right.'

'I'll try not to have to,' said Gareth. 'I'll be as quick as I can. You stay here and look at the view.'

'I don't like it,' said Alwena. 'It's too steep. I feel as though I'm going to fall off.'

Gareth stared at her in disappointment. You'd have thought the twentieth-century equivalent of Ann Jones-Mortimer would have had more imagination. Then, as she tried to stand up, he realised that not only were her hands strangely bent but her whole body was stooped and somehow lopsided. He reached out and caught her elbow to help her. She was even smaller and thinner than he had thought.

'I could lift you down, if you like,' he said. 'At least to

103

that clearing. Piggy back, like. You could wait there. It's flat there.'

'All right,' she whispered. 'Thank you.'

She let Gareth help her onto a flat rock from where she could reach to put her arms round his neck. He bent forwards to lift her onto his back. She was very light.

'Is that okay?'

He could feel her small body palpitating nervously. Her feet twitched.

'Can you bend your legs a bit? Then I can get my arm round and hold you up. Okay?'

'Yes,' she whispered.

'Cling on, then. Don't let that dog trip me up, will you?'

He heard a very nervous, breathy noise that might have been a laugh. Supporting her with his right hand and steadying himself with his left he climbed very carefully down the rocks to the clearing, where he let her slide down gently against the tree trunk next to his bicycle. Olwen ran up to it and sniffed it fiercely.

'I'll just nip back for my rucksack.'

When he returned she was still leaning where he had set her down, propped against the tree trunk with that awkward sideways stoop.

'Is this your stick?'

She nodded tiredly.

'Shall I leave it with you, or will I need it to liven up the donkey?' It was like trying to tease a ten-year-old, but when she blushed she looked older.

'You might need it,' she conceded with a faint giggle.

'I'll try not to be long,' said Gareth. 'But I warn you,

I'm not used to donkeys. Not four-legged ones anyway. My two brothers qualify, sometimes. What did you say his name was?'

'His name's Bedwyr.'

'Okay, Bedwyr, here I come.' He brandished the stick and the dog lead at Alwena in farewell. 'See you later.'

The track was easier to find than it had been last time. Not surprising, thought Gareth, all the traffic that's been up it lately. It was still steep, though. *And* slippery. He grabbed at a sapling. Going down was always worse than going up. That donkey had better be sure-footed.

It was crazy, really, trying to carry the girl down on a donkey. Much better to go straight to her parents and tell them where she was. Let them rescue her. She'd never know. She'd just think he hadn't been able to catch the donkey.

He thought about Alwena. Then he thought about Roscoe Morgan. Alwena didn't want her father to know she had found the garden. He, Gareth, didn't want Roscoe Morgan to know he had found the garden either. Besides, you didn't shop people to their parents, whoever they were and whatever they had done.

So, where was that donkey?

*   *   *

'I fell,' said Alwena to her parents, ages later. 'Bedwyr saved me. He and Olwen brought me home.'

It was almost true.

'You know you're not supposed to go into the woods,' said her father. 'You don't know how frantic we've been. We've been searching all over the place for you. We were just about to phone 999 to get help. You've given us the fright of our lives—' He was almost shouting. He hugged Alwena until she yelped in protest. 'Come inside and get warm—look at your lovely new jacket—'

'Put me down, Dad,' said Alwena. 'I'm all right.' She thought of the careful way Gareth had lifted her onto Bedwyr's back and wanted to cry.

'Go and give Bedwyr some water and a haynet, Roscoe,' said Alwena's mother. 'I'll look after Alwena. What she needs is a hot drink.'

'I want you to tell me exactly where you went, so we can fence it off,' said her father. 'And you must promise never, never to go off on your own again.'

'Put me down, Dad, you're hurting me.'

'Put her down, Roscoe,' said her mother. 'Go and see to Bedwyr. It's quite clear she isn't hurt. She's just tired.'

'Can I give Bedwyr a carrot, please?'

'You *may*.' Her mother smiled. 'Oh dear, look at your jacket. It's a good thing it's machine washable. Take it off. *Careful*.' She caught Alwena as she slid awkwardly to the ground from her father's arms. He said, 'I'll see to the donkey. We'll talk about what happened later,' and left the room, slamming the door.

'What's the time?' Alwena asked her mother.

'It's just after six. It's a good thing you're back. The clocks go back on Saturday night. This time next week it would have been dark.' Her mother spoke in a cheerful, matter-of-fact tone but Alwena understood what she was really saying. If she had not come home before dark, her father really would have had all the emergency services out.

106

'Are you hungry?'

'Yes, but I must feed Olwen.'

'I'll feed her. You sit down and rest.'

Alwena allowed herself to be fed, bathed and put to bed. She allowed her father to carry her upstairs. He tucked her in, then sat on the edge of the bed and said, 'Now, can you remember where you got lost?'

'No,' she said, pulling the duvet closer over herself.

'Was it down by the river? Try to think, Alwena. We've got to make it safe. You could have been swept away.'

'I don't know.'

'How did Bedwyr find you? How did you manage to get on his back?'

'I found him, he didn't find me,' said Alwena, thinking quickly. 'There was a patch of good grass he'd found. I climbed on a rock to get on him.' She kept her face well under the duvet. She was not used to lying. 'It was quite easy to get on him,' she said. 'It's not as if he's very big. He's not as big as a pony.'

'What time was this? You shouldn't have stayed out so long.'

'I couldn't find Olwen.' That at least was true, sort of. 'I thought she'd got trapped.'

'You should have come and fetched me,' said her father. 'What would have happened if you'd broken a leg? You might have been out all night! We might never have found you!'

Alwena said nothing.

'I blame myself,' said her father. 'I know I haven't had so much time for you lately. There's been so much to do with the Trust. So many meetings.'

'I don't mind, Dad.'

'You must promise to stay within sight of the house in the future. Alwena, do you promise?'

'I'm tired,' said Alwena.

'Alwena, do you promise?'

'I didn't get lost on purpose,' said Alwena. 'You can't promise not to get lost when you don't do it on purpose. How can you?'

'That's not what I asked,' said her father. 'I hope you're not getting up to anything deceitful, Alwena.'

'I'm not doing anything!' said Alwena. 'Chance would be a fine thing!'

'Leave her alone, Roscoe,' said her mother, coming into the bedroom. 'Our supper's ready. I've been calling you.'

'Sorry,' said Alwena's father. 'Sorry, Alwena, I don't mean to bully you. It's myself I'm angry with, not you. If anything had happened to you!'

He kissed her goodnight. Alwena waited until she had heard both her parents go downstairs, and heaved a sigh of relief.

She didn't want to go to sleep. She wasn't a bit tired. She wanted to think about every second of that afternoon, to live through it all over again.

It wouldn't come in the right order. The bit that came back most vividly, most urgently, was the last bit, as she clung with all her might to Bedwyr's woolly back, arms round his neck, legs hanging, toes tucked into his tummy. Eyes squeezed shut. If she'd felt dizzy as she looked at the view from the Child's Garden, it was nothing to her terror as Bedwyr carried her down through the woods. Bedwyr, who normally never trotted if he could help it, had trotted determinedly all the way, lurching and staggering on the steep bits, then recovering himself. It had felt as through she was falling head first, buffeted from rock to rock. How she had managed to stay on his back she would never know.

He had reached the north drive far ahead of Gareth, stopping immediately. Alwena had slithered to the ground and sat there like a drunk. She badly wanted to be sick. Olwen rushed up a minute later and began to lick her face, her tail wagging frantically.

Then Gareth appeared, swinging on saplings down the last twenty yards of the path like Tarzan, fair hair flying.

'Look at you!' he said. 'Legless! Ew, he shot off, didn't he? Frightened the life out of me! I never thought you'd stick on! Are you okay?'

She took a deep, shaky breath and nodded, but when she tried to speak her voice stuck in her throat and she began to cry.

Gareth squatted down beside her and patted her shoulder uncertainly. 'You've had a shock,' he said. 'P'raps I'd better carry you home.'

'No—no—I'll be fine—' Blinking and sniffing furiously she scrabbled about, trying to get to her feet. Gareth caught her gently by her elbows and helped her to stand up, holding Bedwyr by the dog lead clipped round his neck so that she could support herself against him.

'Awkward old thing, isn't he,' said Gareth. 'I thought I'd never get him up that path.'

'And now you've got to go all the way back up there.'

'Ah well, it'll keep me fit.'

'I've made you very late. Shall you get into trouble?'

'Na, I'll live. Don't worry about me.'

Then he had smiled, a kind, open smile which made his mouth turn up at the corners. He had grey eyes. Alwena had looked away quickly, pressing her face against Bedwyr's neck.

'Do you want to get on his back again?'

She shook her head. 'No—no, I can walk. I can lean on him, he doesn't mind that. It's not far.'

'I'll come with you if you like.'

'No! No, really—'

Then she had made herself look into those grey eyes and say, 'Thank you very much for helping me. I don't know what I'd have done, if you hadn't turned up just then.'

'Knight in shining armour, eh?'

'You won't forget, will you,' she had entreated. 'Not to tell anyone.'

'I don't particularly want people to know, myself. That I've been trespassing and that. Your Dad doesn't like me as it is.'

True. Her father couldn't stand Gareth, and she'd been just as prejudiced herself. She couldn't bear to think of the awful things she had thought about him.

'Ta-ra, then. See you.' He'd turned back to the path, looked up with a groan, waved, and was gone.

Lying in bed, the sense of loss she had experienced as he disappeared into the rhododendrons swept over her again. She felt she would happily go through the whole ordeal again just to re-live that moment when he had smiled at her.

110

She tried to conjure up his face in her mind. He had grey eyes, and wonderful thick, fair eyelashes, and when he smiled his mouth turned up at the corners, and his teeth were white and square.

Yet he hadn't stared at her, particularly.

He must have noticed her, of course. If there had been nothing wrong with her there wouldn't have been any problem about getting down from the garden; she would simply have climbed down as she had climbed up. But she was who she was, Alwena Morgan, with rheumatoid arthritis, and she'd been exhausted and terribly frightened. If it hadn't been for Gareth she didn't know what she would have done.

It had so very *nice*, the way he had helped her. No horrified noises, just, 'Shout if I'm hurting you.' Those few moments when she'd clung to his broad back—he was strong, she'd felt quite comfortable and safe. The back of his parka was stencilled with a big white arrow and the slogan 'Maximum R & B'. It had a bit of fur round the hood which had tickled her nose. She wished her own parka was made of that faded green cotton, not the gaudy colours she and her father had chosen to be cheerful.

The look on his face when he came out of the bushes and saw her sitting there! He'd mistaken her for the Child! He'd been terrified! His face had gone quite slack, as though his brain had stopped. Alwena giggled into her pillow. She'd been quite indignant. 'I'm not *her*,' she'd said. I bet the real Ann Jones-Mortimer was quite indignant as well, she thought, being mistaken for me. How funny it would have been if she had stepped out from behind a rock and said so.

111

'*I'm* Ann Jones-Mortimer and you're both trespassing in my garden!'

Alwena almost wished she had, so that she could have a look at the girl and see what was wrong with her. Not a lot, if she could climb that path on a regular basis. Alwena remembered her long climb up the steep wood, prod, step, prod, her heart almost bursting with the effort. I did jolly well, she thought with surprise.

She thought carefully about this. Perhaps it wasn't such a steep path, it just seemed like it to her, because she was so bent and frail. But no, Gareth thought it was a really hard climb as well, and he was tall and straight and fit. So that was good, really, that she had climbed all that way on her own.

She'd stayed on Bedwyr's back all the way down. 'I never thought you'd stick on!' Gareth had said. But she had. Did that mean that she could still ride? Ride properly, that was, not just sit in the saddle and be led about. Might it be possible to ride a pony again one day?

It was confusing to start wishing and hoping like this. She had always forbidden herself to daydream about riding again. It was too upsetting, because it seemed too impossible.

Her father would never allow it anyway.

He would be furious if he knew she and Gareth had found the garden. He'd probably blame Gareth for getting her into danger, not praise him for getting her out of it. It was a miracle he hadn't spotted them, those last few moments on the north drive, if he'd been out searching as long as he'd said. He had obviously been concentrating on the river—in future she would have to be careful not to let him catch her near the path to the garden.

Not that she had any intention of climbing up there again. It was a frightening place. Steep, and all that sky. No sign of any summerhouse, either. The Child could keep it.

You can have the garden, and I'll have the house, she told Ann Jones-Mortimer. As she dozed off to sleep she thought, perhaps I'll show Gareth round the house, if he comes again.

*   *   *

On Saturday morning at breakfast Alwena's father said, 'T. J. says he's got friend Gareth coming again today, but I don't suppose he'll show up in this weather.'

The sunny, frosty weather had broken and it was raining heavily. The kitchen windows were steamed up and the old quarry-tiled floor sweated with damp.

Alwena's heart jumped. Gareth had almost stopped being a real person in her mind; he was nearly a myth, a person in history like Ann Jones-Mortimer. She had been having long mental conversations with them both all week. Her parents had put her dreamy mood down to exhaustion following her ordeal on Tuesday. She had been encouraged to stay indoors and rest, and had even been let off swimming. Yet despite her fatigue, somehow, at another level, she hadn't felt so well for ages. It was as though she had quarts of extra blood pumping through her veins.

'Well, if he does turn up,' said her mother, 'there's no way I'm going to let you push him outside to eat his

113

sandwiches on a day like this. We'll give him a proper lunch.'

'He's getting to be a bit of a nuisance,' said Alwena's father. 'We don't want to encourage him. Besides, he upsets Alwena.'

Alwena's mother said patiently, 'I don't know why you're behaving as though this rather ordinary, nice, teenage boy, who's clearly got a positive interest in the house and is disposed to be helpful, is some kind of dangerous wild beast.'

'I told you, I don't trust him,' said her father grumpily. 'He's got an insolent look about him.'

Unexpectedly, her mother began to laugh. 'I know what it is,' she said. 'You're missing David. You used to say exactly the same sort of thing about him.'

'Not at all,' said Alwena's father angrily. 'David's a pain in the neck, like all undergraduates. Thinks he knows it all. But we know where we are with David. He's got some respect for the place, at least. Besides, he's Alwena's brother and he knows how ill she's been. Not like this young—'

'I don't mind,' said Alwena, finishing her boiled egg and pushing her spoon through the bottom of the shell.

She could not let her father go on about Gareth like that any more. He was her friend. Well, not her friend, exactly, but he was on her side. She owed him some loyalty.

'Not like this young vandal,' her father continued as though she had not spoken.

Alwena said, a little louder, 'I don't mind if he has lunch with us.'

Both her parents looked at her in disbelief.

'Well, if it's only him,' she mumbled.

'Goodness,' said her mother. 'Are you sure?'

'Yes,' she said. 'I don't mind if it's just one. And not those girls. Can I have another piece of toast?'

'You may,' said her mother. A very cheerful smile came over her face. 'Good for you, Alwena.'

'I bet he won't come,' said her father, stamping off to his office.

Chapter Eight

'Five years!' said Gareth's father. 'No way!'

In the Careers Room at Ysgol Abercoed the fluorescent light flickered. In the darkness outside the window the sodium street lights were reflected in the puddles on the playground. It was cold; the school's heating was switched off at three thirty every afternoon as an economy measure.

Gareth slouched in his chair, hugging his parka round himself and ignoring his mother's disapproving looks. She sat up very straight, listening deferentially to what the Careers teacher, Mr Denis Thomas, had to say.

Denis Thomas had a black beard, a brown corduroy suit, red braces and a Cardiff accent, none of which were helping him to be taken seriously by Gareth's father.

Gareth's mother said, 'He seems very keen on buildings. He's got posters of bridges and buildings all over his bedroom walls.'

'How much do you reckon five years at University is going to cost us?' demanded Gareth's father belligerently. 'Do you think we're made of money or what? And what would there be to show for it in the end? A stuck-up little fart with letters after his name and no practical use to anybody.'

'Architects can do pretty well for themselves,' said Denis Thomas vaguely, peering at the top sheet of a bundle of papers fastened together with a green plastic bulldog clip. 'It's an international profession. Look at that woman who designed the Cardiff Bay Opera House.'

Oh God, thought Gareth. Please don't let Dad get started on the Opera House.

'We need good architects in Wales, Mr Lloyd,' said Denis Thomas, making an effort.

'We need good plumbers,' said Gareth's father. 'Good electricians as well, by the look of that light. Practical people with practical skills.'

'I quite agree,' said Denis Thomas heartily. 'The very people architects depend on. Any son of yours who became an architect would know how important that was, Mr Lloyd.'

Fair play, he is doing his best, thought Gareth.

'Well,' said Gareth's father, after a moment. 'If I thought it was anything more than a daydream, it would be different.'

'Well,' said Denis Thomas, 'he'll need good A Level grades, of course.'

'And what do you think his chances are with his A Levels, Mr Thomas?' asked his mother, leaning forward.

116

'Hopeless, unless he gets his finger out.'

Gareth was winded by the Career teacher's unexpected bluntness. He sat up indignantly.

'Honestly, Gareth, you do let yourself down,' said his mother. 'After doing so well in your GCSEs, too.'

'Of course, it's early days,' said Denis Thomas. 'It can sometimes be hard to get yourself going in the Sixth Form, I mean Year Twelve. After the pressure of GCSEs. I will say, none of his teachers think he lacks the ability.'

'I don't know where they get that idea from,' said Gareth's father, 'if he's anything like he is at home when he's at school. Half asleep, most of the time.'

'He can't have been asleep when he did his GCSEs,' his mother pointed out. 'He got six As and three Bs.'

'Unfortunately,' said Denis Thomas, tilting his chair and taking a quick look at his watch, 'it can sometimes be counter-productive for people to do too well with their GCSEs. They think they can sit back and let the A Levels look after themselves.'

Whose side is he flaming well on? thought Gareth, clenching his hands on the side of his chair. He felt like throwing it at Denis Thomas.

'Well, he's not messing about for two years,' said Gareth's father. 'He can either get stuck into his studying or finish school and come and be apprenticed to me. I'm not carrying any passengers in my house. It's not even as if he's interested in sport.'

If he thought I was likely to make the All Wales Under 21 Football team we wouldn't be going through any of this, thought Gareth. Nor if it was rugby neither.

'I've got nothing against him being an architect if he's

really serious about it,' said his father. 'But why can't you be apprenticed to it, like you can to a plumber? Why does it have to take five years at University?'

'Ah well, now you're asking,' said Denis Thomas. 'There's no denying it's an expensive business these days. There may be some scholarships, perhaps.'

'I'm not saying we couldn't find some of the money,' began Gareth's father.

'But he'll need A Levels whatever he does, won't he, Mr Thomas,' interrupted his mother. 'He won't get anywhere without them.'

'Quite. Absolutely right—mind you, there is the BTec option of course.'

'BTec!' exploded Gareth, insulted to the core of his being. 'I'm not doing any bloody BTecs!'

'You can qualify as an architectural technician that way,' said Denis Thomas, flipping through a wad of computer printout. 'I think that's what they call it. Ah, here we are. You'd need to go for a trainee post, and go to college on day release. Or you can do your A Levels and go for an HND after that. Or you could do a degree in architectural technology. That takes just three years, but I believe you can do it part-time if you want. Quite a few people qualify that way, it says here.'

'That's more like it,' said Gareth's father. 'Practical, on-the-job training. I can make sense of that. Then he can pay his own way through architecture college when he's older if that's what he wants.'

Stuck in an office behind a drawing board for the next ten years? thought Gareth. No way.

'You'd be earning straight away,' said his father.

'You'll be wanting a car next year, won't you? First sense I've heard for months. He'll be able to take his girl-friend out without cadging money off me.' He grinned and winked at Denis Thomas as though recognising an ally.

'I don't cadge money off you,' muttered Gareth through clenched teeth. Elin was someone else he felt like strangling. She had adopted a strategy of working her way into Gareth's affections by captivating her father, and the old fool had fallen for it. He'd been buying her lager and limes in the pub last Saturday night as though she was his daughter-in-law already.

'Wait a minute,' said Mrs Lloyd. 'We went through all this business last year before he did his GCSEs. I didn't hear any talk of BTecs then. You were all for him doing his A Levels and going on to college. Four A Levels he's doing. It's not fair to pull him out before he's hardly got going.'

'I'm not subsidising a layabout! I'm fed up with him as well, he's getting too proud to live. Who does he think he is?'

Gareth dropped his head forward and thrust his hands wearily through his hair. As usual in these confrontations he could think of nothing to say. The room was cold but he felt stifled. He longed to be at the Plas, standing on a knoll in the windy park drawing the house. Or up in the Child's Garden. The sunset that last Tuesday had been magnificent. He hadn't been able to resist climbing up to the garden for one last look, with the result that he had forgotten to retrieve his bicycle.

'Well, say something, Gareth, if it's only goodbye,' Denis Thomas was saying.

Gareth sat up, tossing back his hair. The Careers

teacher was chewing the insides of his cheeks as though trying not to laugh. His mother said crossly, 'If you can't speak up for yourself I don't know why I'm bothering.'

'Sorry,' mumbled Gareth. 'Sorry, Mum.' He looked at his father helplessly.

'You've got to let him do his A Levels, Bryn,' said his mother.

'Well, I don't know—if he can be a trainee—'

'Why don't we see how his mocks go?' said Denis Thomas. 'If he ploughs his mocks, you can do what you like with him, Mr Lloyd, and I'll be right there to help you.'

'It's a deal,' said Gareth's father. His face began to relax. 'Do you have many like him?' he asked, jerking his head at his son.

'Oh yes,' said Denis Thomas. 'Dear me, yes.'

'He'd better stop mucking about, then. Mind, I'm not sure, even now. There'd be no harm in him writing off to ask about being a trainee, would there? There's plenty of architects' firms in Aberystwyth. Lampeter as well. I know one or two of them myself—I could have a word.'

'Good idea,' said Denis Thomas. 'You could ask about holiday jobs as well, Gareth. Be good experience for you.'

'Okay,' said Gareth. Anything for a quiet life, he thought. Mind you, a holiday job might not be a bad idea, if he could get one.

'In the meantime, Gareth,' said his mother, looking more cheerful as the atmosphere relaxed, 'You've got to work harder. Mr Thomas has got a point. You can't take your A Levels for granted, they're harder than GCSEs.'

'I am working hard,' said Gareth. 'I got an A for my half term project for Art.'

120

'Oh, so he's not been struck dumb after all. I was beginning to wonder!' said his father.

'Oh yes, Miss Davies said she was very pleased with it. A marvellous set of drawings of that old mansion, I've forgotten what it's called,' said Denis Thomas. 'Did he show them to you?'

'He's obsessed with that bloody place,' said Gareth's father. 'I'm fed up with it. He lost his bike there last week, so instead of trying to find it he took mine. Brought it back in a hell of a state.'

Here we go again, thought Gareth.

'That reminds me,' said Denis Thomas hastily. 'There's a History project to do with it coming off as well, isn't there, Gareth?' He leafed through his bundle of papers. 'T. J. was telling me—ah yes, here we are— he's been impressed with Gareth's approach to the project. He's obviously thinking about it, he's shown quite a lot of commitment and he hasn't been afraid to ask awkward questions.'

Saved, thought Gareth, seeing his father start to grin.

'That's what T. J. said, is it?' said his father. 'You hear that, Gareth? Not afraid to ask awkward questions, eh! And who was the one who was asking the awkward questions I'd like to know!'

'Well, Dad, I thought you made some important points,' said Gareth.

'You'll be wanting me to sit the bloody exams for you next,' said his father.

*   *   *

Two hours later Gareth went to his room, lay on his bed and plugged in his Walkman, his ears still hot from the ticking-off his mother had given him as soon as his father had disappeared to the pub for his ten-thirty pint.

'Your father works all hours God sends to keep you boys, he's out by half past seven every morning, Saturdays as well. I don't blame him for getting mad when you mooch about with that stupid smile on your face. He's not against you wanting to get on, but he can't stand to see you not working hard.'

Gareth sighed. A right sermon it had been. He supposed he deserved it. The trouble was, he found his father so tiring. His quick-tempered energy, his alternate flashes of anger and humour wore Gareth out. You never had time to think anything through. You couldn't discuss anything with him, he could never listen for long enough.

Lacks concentration, thought Gareth. Like me. Ho ho.

Funny how different he was when it came to plumbing. He could sit for hours, thoughtfully nibbling his thumbnail, when trying to work out how to lay a pipe in a house where the drains hadn't been dug deep enough. He would get Gareth to draw diagrams and calculate water pressures, and would listen patiently while Gareth explained his calculations.

Perhaps that was why he was not keen on Gareth going to University: he had been counting on him to join the business. So he was doing his best to scotch his son's ambitions to keep him here in Abercoed. Selfish sod.

Gareth knew this was unfair. He loved his father; he even liked him, most of the time. But you couldn't talk to him. He didn't have any imagination. He'd never wanted to get away.

Nobody wanted Gareth to get away, not really. His Dad didn't. Elin didn't. The school didn't care either way, he was just one more local hick passing through their hands, never likely to make anything of himself.

He swung restlessly to his feet and stared out of his bedroom window at the sodium-lit estate road. A car swung into the drive of the house opposite and the automatic doors of the garage opened. The car drove in and the garage door slid down again with a clunk. A light went on in the house.

That was what his father wanted for him. House, car, garage with automatic doors, telly, Elin ordering clothes out of mail order catalogues. It was depressing. This claustrophobic, semi-detached twentieth century, he thought. Where had he heard that recently? It was true.

Roscoe Morgan. It was Roscoe Morgan, in the library at the Plas, going on about how people were afraid to have big ideas these days.

It made Gareth uncomfortable to think that he might be lining up on the same side as Roscoe Morgan against his father. There was anger, and a kind of meanness about Roscoe Morgan, as though he were jealous of everybody. He wouldn't want him for a father for all the great houses in Europe.

Gareth didn't often feel sorry for girls, but he felt sorry for Alwena.

*   *   *

Gareth couldn't make out why she had been so desperate for her father not to find out where she had been that day he had helped her down from the garden. Until last Saturday when, still using his father's bike, he had cycled over to Plas Idaleg for another session in the library and found himself meeting the whole Morgan family.

It had been awful. Roscoe Morgan had done nothing but glare while his wife made a fuss about Gareth being mad to come out in this wet weather. She'd insisted that he take off his parka and leave it to be dried out in the kitchen. Alwena had sat silently, not looking at him, bent fowards in her chair by the fire and holding on to the dog Olwen's collar. T. J. sat next to her, filling his pipe and observing them all with amused sharp eyes as though all *his* plans were going very nicely, thank you.

Lunch had been worse. There was no getting out of it. Mrs Morgan made cheerful conversation, to which only T. J. responded. Roscoe Morgan helped Alwena to the table as though she were a total cripple and nagged on about draughts. Gareth had kept his eyes on his plate all through the meal, which at least made it quite easy to give no hint of his having met Alwena before.

She had hardly spoken except to say, 'I'm all right, Dad,' in a low voice, every time he asked her if she was warm enough, or if she needed her chair moving forward a bit. Gareth could sense both Mrs Morgan's suppressed irritation and Alwena's embarrassment.

If it weren't for her father you wouldn't notice anything in particular was wrong with her, at least not while she was sitting at the table. Lots of people held their knives and forks bent inwards like that.

No wonder she climbed up to the garden, thought Gareth. She was trying to escape.

After lunch T. J. said to Alwena, 'Would you like to come and help us for a while, Alwena? We've found an interesting book of trees, haven't we, Gareth? Lovely, hand-tinted engravings, you know. We are lucky to have it, a dealer would have torn out all the plates and framed them. Fetch a fortune in an antique shop.'

Before Alwena could reply Roscoe Morgan had interrupted. 'It doesn't do Alwena good to spend too much time in the library. It's dusty. She has to be careful of her lungs.'

Alwena had opened her mouth, then closed it again. For the first time that day she allowed her eyes to meet Gareth's. She flushed. Then she said,

'I do my lessons in the library.'

Her father replied at once, 'Yes, and I'm not so sure it's a very good idea now that we're doing so much work on the books.' His tone implied that this activity was nothing to do with him, that it was being imposed on him by T. J. and Gareth.

Alwena set her mouth. Gareth waited for her to speak, but she remained silent. She looked down at the table. Mrs Morgan smiled at Gareth. 'Why don't you put the book on one side, and we'll come along and look at it later,' she suggested.

At the end of the afternoon he had had to return to the kitchen to collect his parka. Roscoe Morgan was busy in his office, otherwise Gareth felt sure he would not have been permitted to make his way there unaccompanied.

In the kitchen Alwena was sitting by the kitchen

range, reading. She looked up as he came in. Olwen the dog jumped up with a bark and began to wag her tail. This seemed to give Alwena the courage to smile.

'Here you are!' said Mrs Morgan. She handed him the parka, and watched while he put it on rather as his own mother would have done. Then she had strolled with him through the house to the front entrance where he had left his bicycle. 'At least the rain's let up a bit,' she said.

He had been about to lift his bike down the steps when she had laid a hand on his arm. 'Gareth, I just wanted to say—you mustn't mind my husband.'

'I don't,' he had muttered, wondering what was coming.

'Our daughter,' said Mrs Morgan, 'Alwena has rheumatoid arthritis. She has been ill for a long time. My husband is very protective towards her. You mustn't take it personally.'

Gareth wondered if she was going to suggest that it would be better for him not to come to Plas Idaleg again.

'But I hope you'll keep on coming,' Mrs Morgan had continued. 'You and your friends, if they're still interested. It would be good for all of us. We're very cut off, here at Plas Idaleg. It can be very lonely.'

*   *   *

They're all going slowly mad there, thought Gareth, lying on his bed at home, Jimi Hendrix's guitar screaming unheard in his ears. That's why T. J. got us lot to go there. To stop Plas Idaleg turning into a big, beautiful lunatic asylum.

It would be better when it was turned into this Centre they were talking about. It would let air into the place, open up all those rooms shut off behind their great mahogany doors. Clear all the brambles from the woodland paths and open up those gardens and that view.

He sighed. He could see why this would be better than letting Plas Idaleg remain a hidden, secret place you had to hack your way into. But really, he preferred it secret, especially the garden. He hated the thought of the Child's Garden being open to the public and signposted and featured on *Gardeners' World*. It needed to be wild and remote and a struggle to get to.

Alwena had had to struggle much harder to get there than he had. You could not deny the girl had guts, slogging on long after her strength had failed, until she had reached the garden and found her dog. He had been shocked by her frailty as he had carried her down to the clearing. I should have carried her all the way, he thought now. I could easily have done it. I shouldn't have let her ride that donkey. If she'd fallen off she could have been killed.

He sat up and took off his earphones, shaken by the memory of his thoughtlessness. It jolted him out of all his longing for the wild peace of the garden.

Chapter Nine

The Child didn't have young men coming here, thought Alwena the following Saturday, watching out of the upstairs front window for Gareth to come cycling down the drive. Only old ones.

It had been the same for her until recently, now she came to think of it. The only people who came to Plas Idaleg were old men from the University, architects and archaeologists and historians. And T. J., of course. It must have been quite a disappointment to her father that she had been unable to amaze them with her knowledge of botany and science.

What a good thing I couldn't, she thought. It would have been awful if I had. She did not know quite why she felt like this. She didn't want to be a disappointment to her father, after all. It was very annoying, though, if he wanted her to be like someone who had lived two hundred years ago. Someone he couldn't even bring himself to tell her about. What chance did she have? She felt quite angry with him about it.

'Here he comes,' she said to Olwen, as a male figure came pedalling out of the woods, jumped off his bicycle to lift it across the cattle grid and jumped on again. He cycled quite slowly towards the house, as though taking a good look at it. He swerved a bit as he stared up at the square tower of the campanile.

I wish I had a bike, thought Alwena. I'm sure a bike would be good for me..

A series of clangs and thumps echoed from downstairs as Gareth pushed open the main doors and carried his bicycle inside. Olwen dashed out of the room and down the front staircase, barking excitedly, forcing Alwena to follow her. Alwena was not sorry about this. She had been watching out for Gareth in the hope of meeting him by chance as he arrived, but she hadn't been sure that she wouldn't lose her nerve when the moment came.

She went downstairs slowly, trying to keep her back as straight as possible and not hang onto the banisters. Gareth grinned up at her as he propped his bike against one of the marble columns and bent to fondle Olwen.

'I can't get used to this,' he said. 'It's like parking your bike in church. Or Trafalgar Square,' he added as a pigeon dropping splatted to the floor just missing his shoulder. They both looked up at the pigeons which flapped about in the shadows high above them. Alwena giggled, then stopped herself quickly.

'All this marble!' said Gareth. 'Look at the patterns in the floor, it's all marble!'

'It makes it cold,' said Alwena. 'It must have been a very cold house in the olden days, even when they had fires.'

'Draughty,' agreed Gareth. 'Do you ever light fires in that big fireplace over there?'

'Sometimes. The chimneys aren't safe, Dad says.'

'They won't be, if they don't have fires in them,' said Gareth. He sounded very certain, as though he knew all about chimneys. His father was a plumber, she remembered her father saying. Did plumbers do chimneys as well as bathrooms and toilets?

'The damp gets in them,' said Gareth. She realised he

129

was looking embarrassed. She blushed herself, ashamed that he might think she had been staring at him.

'You got home all right then, that time,' he said after a moment.

'Oh—yes, yes I was fine.' She opened her mouth to thank him all over again, thought better of the idea and closed it.

'Is T. J. here yet?'

'I don't know. He'll be in the library. It's this way.'

'Oh yes, I remember.' He coughed self-consciously. She followed him through the house, hanging back so that he would not notice her awkward walk. Olwen trotted alongside. Thinking hard for something polite to say she came up with, 'It's quite easy to get lost in this house.'

Gareth grinned quickly over his shoulder at her. 'When I first came here I kept wondering what was behind all those doors,' he said. 'I kept thinking they were like trapdoors. Open the wrong one and bang! you were trapped. They were like daring you. I put my hand out, but just as I touched the door knob a dog started barking.'

'Oh,' said Alwena shyly.

'Then when I took my hand away, it stopped.'

Alwena suddenly got the point of the story.

'Frightened me to death, it did. I thought the Hound of the Baskervilles was going to get me.'

Alwena nearly overbalanced as laughter bubbled through her. She leaned against the wall for support. 'That was Olwen,' she said. 'That was you, Olwen! He thought you were a ghost!' Olwen frowned up at her anxiously.

'There's nothing behind the doors,' Alwena told Gareth. 'Only rooms. Look!' She opened the nearest door and Gareth followed her into a large room with long windows along the opposite wall and another large marble fireplace.

'Oh yes, I remember this room, T. J. showed it to us the first time we came here.' It was the Saloon he'd fantasised about squatting in.

'But there are lots more. Look!' She hobbled across the corridor and opened another door, and another; in and out of room after room. Gareth wandered after her, gaping at painted ceilings and marble floors and carved plasterwork. One of the rooms was full of dusty mirrors, hung so that they could see countless ghostly reflections of themselves, with dozens of fireplaces and hundreds of windows reflecting and reflecting to infinity.

The amazed expression on Gareth's face filled Alwena with joy. She waved into one of the mirrors. 'Look,' she cried, 'You can't tell which is me and which is one of my hundred and fifty ghosts.'

'It's crazy,' said Gareth. 'It's fantastic.'

Their laughter gusted with the wind, which blew through the house, slamming doors and setting the aged windows rattling in their frames.

'What the hell do you think you're doing?'

Roscoe Morgan erupted into the mirrored room and stared around him, furious and disconcerted at the sight of so many Alwenas and Gareths. Alwena stopped laughing.

'I was only showing Gareth the Mirror Saloon, Dad,' she said.

'Well, come out. If any of those mirrors get broken we'll be in trouble. You've got no business poking about in all the rooms,' he told Gareth.

'It was me,' said Alwena anxiously. 'I opened the doors. Only to show him. I thought it would be all right, to show him.'

Her father frowned at her. He seemed puzzled as well as angry. He glared at Gareth.

'Windy day!' T. J. Mostyn put his head round the door, unwinding a long, bedraggled scarf from round his neck. 'Did you bring those drawings, my boy?'

'Yes,' said Gareth, 'I'll just go and get them.'

He muttered 'Excuse me,' and slid round Roscoe Morgan out of the room. T. J.'s old cheeks were scarlet with cold. He pulled out a handkerchief and wiped his eyes. 'It's bitter!' he said. 'Gareth's done some very nice drawings of Plas Idaleg, Roscoe. I told him to bring them round to show you.'

Alwena could see that her father was longing to make remarks about Gareth being a nuisance, and it not being a very good idea to encourage him. She was pleased that T. J. had pulled the ground from under his feet.

'Alwena, you'd better run along back to the kitchen,' said her father. 'You'll catch cold with all these doors wide open.'

'But I want to see the drawings!' protested Alwena. 'Anyway, I'm perfectly warm. I'm wearing my parka.'

Her father made an impatient noise, and turned on his heel. T. J. twinkled cheerily at Alwena, laid his hand on her shoulder and walked with her to the library.

A few moments later they all watched as Gareth self-consciously opened the folder he had taken from his rucksack and laid his drawings out on the table one by one. Roscoe Morgan gazed at them for a long time without speaking. T. J. smiled serenely as he took out his pipe and tobacco wallet.

Alwena looked anxiously at her father, wanting him to calm down and stop being angry with Gareth.

At length he said reluctantly, 'They are very good.'

Gareth went red, and muttered something that might have been 'Thanks.'

Her father cleared his throat. 'You've taken a lot of trouble.'

'They're for my Art project,' said Gareth. 'I hope it's all right.'

'Well,' said her father, 'I suppose.' He paused, then added grudgingly, 'The Trustees support the idea of doing educational projects based on Plas Idaleg.'

'I told you he was interested in architecture,' said T. J., prodding tobacco comfortably into the bowl of his pipe.

'It's an interesting place,' said Gareth awkwardly. 'It's got an interesting history, with the lead mines, and the Child and all that.'

Alwena saw her father's expression change. His glance flashed from Alwena to T. J. to Gareth. 'I hope you're not paying any attention to any silly nonsense!' he said. 'Alwena, why don't you go and find your mother, she was looking for you—'

'Oh Dad,' interrupted Alwena. 'Don't be so *silly*. I know all about the Child.'

'The Child? What child?'

'Our Child. The Plas Idaleg Child. Her name's Ann

133

Jones-Mortimer and she was the daughter of Sir Edward Jones-Mortimer and she was good at science and she had arthritis, like me.'

Her father reached clumsily for a chair and sat down slowly. The look of distress on his face frightened Alwena. It was not anger, but shock and a dreadful sadness.

*　　　*　　　*

'She had a curvature of the spine,' said Alwena's mother. 'As far as we know, that is. Her father talks about her spinal disease in his letters. Not like JRA, but some of the symptoms are the same I believe.'

JRA was Juvenile Rheumatoid Arthritis.

'She can't have been all that ill, if she roamed the gardens all the time,' said Alwena. She sat at the kitchen table, sipping a mug of tea, watching her mother prepare supper.

Her mother said, 'Well she probably had her good days and her bad days, like you.'

'What happened to her?'

Alwena's mother stood up from putting potatoes to bake in the oven of the kitchen range. 'They moved away from here,' she said. 'Edward Jones-Mortimer went bankrupt, you've heard T. J. talking about it. I believe they went to Devonshire.'

'Did she get better?'

Her mother paused, then said, 'Well, the climate probably suited her better down there.'

'She wanted to be a scientist,' said Alwena.

'You be grateful that you live in the nineteen nineties

134

and not the seventeen nineties,' said her mother. 'With proper medicine and proper education for everybody. There's no need to model yourself on a girl who lived two hundred years ago.'

'I'm no good at science anyway.'

Her mother laughed. 'Well, you're not *bad* at it. But you're bound to be a bit behind. The sooner you're back at school now, the better.'

Alwena said nothing. She might have known her mother would work the conversation round to that topic.

Later that night as she lay in bed she could hear her parents arguing about it downstairs. As usual they could not get past the matter of Aberystwyth versus Abercoed.

Gareth went to Ysgol Abercoed.

Her father had attended Ysgol Abercoed when he was young; so had her brother David for a year or two, before her father had got the job in the University which entailed moving to Aberystwyth. As a result of the move Alwena had started school in Aberystwyth and had remained there even after the family had moved to Plas Idaleg. Her father claimed that the secondary school in Aberystwyth was superior to the one in Abercoed but her mother said he only said that because it was full of university lecturers' children.

Alwena had heard it all before.

The big advantage of Abercoed as far as her mother was concerned was that the school building was nearly all on ground floor level with no stairs, so it would be easier for Alwena to get about. The big advantage of Abercoed as far as Alwena was concerned was that Gareth went there.

Not for much longer though, if he was in the Sixth Form.

He would be different at school with all his Sixth Form friends around him. All those girls. He was so good-looking, he probably had lots of girlfriends. He wouldn't be as nice with all those girls around. He wouldn't want to be seen giggling with a girl from year whatever it was who was partially disabled.

And yet, what would happen if she did not go back to school? What would become of her?

There was plenty to do here at Plas Idaleg still, of course. She thought of the *Ceredigion* article. There were still all the other gardens it mentioned to find yet. She must try to find more of the old paths, perhaps make a map.

There had to be a role for her at Plas Idaleg. Her father wanted her to have one. He wanted her to be his clever daughter when all the archaeologists and architects started coming. Once he got over his fear of allowing her to explore on her own he would be pleased that she had shown such initiative. 'Alwena knows the estate backwards,' he would say proudly. 'She's the spirit of Plas Idaleg.'

Lying in bed, Alwena shivered. Things hadn't been the same since she had heard the true facts about the Child. Ann Jones-Mortimer. Ann Jones-Mortimer's father had regarded *her* as the spirit of Plas Idaleg.

It was as though Alwena's father wanted her to live a life that somebody else had lived already.

No, no, that wasn't fair. He just worried about her and wanted her to get better, to grow up into a daughter he could be proud of, the same as the Child's father had felt about her.

Perhaps the Child had got just as impatient with him at times as Alwena did with her father.

Oh, I *do*, Alwena imagined the Child saying. He won't let me go *anywhere* on my own. I must always have servants with me, even when I'm really well!

Alwena giggled into the duvet and pulled it over her head to drown out her parents' voices. She began to tell herself a story in which she and the Child met secretly to explore the estate. They would discover all the lost gardens, to the amazement of Alwena's father. She tried to work out a part for Gareth to play in this story, but it would not come right. It was as though he had arrived too early. She was still trying to puzzle out why this should be so when she fell asleep.

In the early hours of the morning she awoke with a bump, flailing her arms to get her balance. Her eyes flew open. She gasped for breath. It was dark, whereas in her dream it had been light.

The voices were still in her head.

'Look, we can fly! Hold my hand, Alwena, we can fly!'

They had been in the garden, standing on the edge of the precipice, gazing with wonder into the far distance. There were mountains, and forests, and oceans, and glittering cities.

They had run to the garden together, calling and laughing to each other. It was summer; all the plants that grew over the rocks were in flower. Birds and rabbits darted about. Alwena and the Child played tag up and down the garden, shrieking with delight.

'I'm really well!' cried the Child. 'I'm really well!' She ran to the edge of the rock and held out her arms to the sun.

'Look, we can fly! Hold my hand, Alwena!' Alwena raced after her and caught her hand. They soared into the air. 'We're flying!' cried the Child. 'We're flying!' Then everything turned upside-down and Alwena felt herself falling at top speed, the landscape swinging round and the tops of the trees rushing nearer and nearer.

Her legs twitched violently as she clutched the edge of her bed. She felt seasick. Her ears were popping, as though she really had fallen hundreds of metres out of the sky.

She was there, Alwena thought, shivering. The Child was there. In my dream. She thought hard, trying to recall what the Child had looked like, what the garden had looked like, but already the details were eluding her, dissolving, leaving only the sense of a great precipice and a terrible spinning fall.

It was a relief to sit up, to slide her bare feet out onto the rug at the side of the bed and feel the wooden floorboards underneath. She scrambled clumsily into her slippers and dressing gown and pulled herself across the room to sit by the window against the huge, old-fashioned iron radiator, pressing her knees against its solid warmth. She sat there until it got light, frightened of going back to bed in case she had that dream all over again.

For the rest of the day she felt near to tears of gratitude for the solidness of the ground under her feet. The kitchen tiles, the cobbled yard, the parkland turf. But the dream haunted her.

Chapter Ten

November passed slowly. The fog settled on the Cardiganshire hills; on Abercoed and Plas Idaleg, and on all the villages and hill farms and deserted lead mines that lay between them.

Gareth's bicycle still lay where he had left it on the path to the Child's Garden. He imagined it getting rustier and rustier, slowly disappearing under a curtain of bright green moss. He told his father he had left it at Llŷr Hir's farm, and Llŷr's father would drop it off next time he came to Abercoed with the Land Rover. To inject some truth into this story he planned to go to Plas Idaleg again to retrieve the bike as soon as possible, but not on a Saturday when Llŷr or any of the others from the A Level group might be there, and certainly not while the weather was so foggy.

The fog got onto T. J.'s chest, and into Gareth's head. It seemed to clog his entire system, weighing him down so that his shoulders sagged and his head drooped, causing his father to ask if he was studying the pavements and gutters of Abercoed for his latest A Level project.

'And have you written to those architects yet?'

No, he hadn't, was the answer to that. Something in his gut stopped him, although in his rational mind he could see the sense of making contact with local firms, and finding out what architects actually did instead of just dreaming about fantastic buildings. The summer job idea was a good one too, though it killed him to admit it. But it was as though by bending to his father's will he would be stepping onto the inevitable road to semi-detached purgatory, sealing his fate as surely as if he were to stop trying to keep Elin out of his life.

Not that that was easy. She was too available and he was too well, polite, he tried to convince himself. He didn't want to hurt her feelings. Too lazy, you mean, his conscience retorted brutally.

To avoid her, he stopped going out at weekends. He shut himself in his room and tried to work on his History project, reading a library book on the history of Cardiganshire. He helped his father draw up some plumbing estimates for a local builder, and fell out with his brothers. He at last spotted his chance to get the map of the Plas Idaleg estate photocopied one day when Menna Williams was not on duty at the copy shop. The man who ran the video and copy shop was an incomer, the map meant nothing special to him but he still pored over it with interest, telling Gareth he was wise to get it copied. 'These old maps fetch quite a lot these days if they're in good condition. You want to get it framed,' he said chattily, while Gareth looked furtively over his shoulder in case T. J. Mostyn should pass by and come into the shop to see what Gareth was doing.

'You haven't been to the Plas lately,' said T. J. to him after a history lesson a few weeks later. 'You've been missed.'

'It's been too foggy,' said Gareth. 'I've been helping Dad.' Like hell I've been missed, he thought. That Roscoe Morgan is missing me like a hole in the head.

'Haven't you noticed the withdrawal symptoms, T. J.?' said Llŷr Hir who was listening in. 'He's been in a filthy temper for weeks. He's missing the mansion. He needs a Plas Idaleg fix. He wishes he lived there, like one of the gentry.'

'No, I don't,' said Gareth.

'Yes, you do. You don't think about anything else. You walk round in a dream most of the time.'

'Well, you were quite interested yourself when you heard about the ghost.'

'A very nice little ghost,' said T. J., picking up his books and folders and hoisting them under his arm. 'And she could do with a bit of company too.' He gave them a cheerful nod and hurried out of the classroom.

'What's he on about?'

Gareth said, 'I dunno.' Then he added reluctantly, 'There's a girl. A daughter for that chap.'

'What chap?'

'Roscoe Morgan. Those doors banging. It was her.'

'Oh! A girl!' said Llŷr. He began to grin. 'How old?'

'Don't get carried away,' said Gareth. 'She's been ill. She walks with a limp.'

'I thought that was the girl T. J. told us about, in the olden days.'

'This is another one.'

'What's her name?'

'I've forgotten.'

'Oh ho,' said Llŷr. 'Does Elin know? I ask myself.'

'Shut up!'

'I see, he doesn't want to tell. I shall have to cycle over one of these Saturdays and take a look for myself.'

Gareth said, 'Well, make sure you go to the servants' entrance then.'

Llŷr chose to take this as an insult. He grabbed Gareth by the lapels and pushed him against the wall. Gareth lost his temper and hit him on the nose. Before they could set about one another any further they were being separated by the PE teacher and a couple of lads from Year Thirteen on their way in from football training. Blood poured from Llŷr's nose.

'Are you all right?' Gareth asked him afterwards as they made their way to the refectory for lunch.

'You didn't have to go mad,' said Llŷr, taking the wad of toilet tissue from his nose and looking at the scarlet stains. 'You know I get nose bleeds.'

'Sorry,' said Gareth. 'It's this blasted fog. I can't see out.'

*   *   *

'What does Pensile mean?' asked Gareth, the following Saturday, frowning as he read the *Ceredigion* article.

'It means Hanging,' said Alwena. 'I looked it up in the dictionary.'

'It's a hanging garden all right,' said Gareth. 'You practically need safety belts. There ought to be a cable car.'

'Oh yes,' agreed Alwena fervently. She was still haunted by that awful falling dream.

They were in the Octagon Library, just the two of them, sitting at the table. Dusty sunlight filtered through the lantern. Alwena could not get over the luck of Gareth turning up again on the very day her father had gone to Aberystwyth to give a lecture on the Plas Idaleg project at the National Library. T. J. had gone too.

142

Her mother had been just as pleased to see him. 'Oh good, here's some company for you, Alwena. Make him some coffee.' And she had disappeared into her darkroom.

'How did you get here?' Alwena had asked Gareth, seeing no bicycle parked in the front hall.

'My Dad dropped me by T. J.'s house. He's had to go to Telford for some parts.'

He had offered to drive him all the way to the house but Gareth had managed to put him off. His heart had sunk at the prospect of his father's curiosity being aroused. Give him half a chance and he'd be nosing round the house advising Roscoe Morgan on its restoration.

'I must pick up my bike. Out of the wood,' said Gareth to Alwena. 'If it hasn't fallen to bits by now.'

'How did you come to leave it there?'

'I was exploring. That first time I found the garden. There was a way in from the top road. Near the church. Hang on.' He pulled the Ordnance Survey map out of his rucksack and opened it.

'A map!' said Alwena. 'Where did you find this?'

Gareth cursed himself. He thought of saying, 'I found it in the second-hand shop in Abercoed.' He gave Alwena a guilty look. 'It was in one of those boxes of books we were sorting out,' he said. 'I borrowed it. I wasn't going to keep it.'

'I've never seen a really old map,' said Alwena, leaning over the table to look at it. 'Dad's got some in his office but I never get a proper chance to look at them. The really old ones are in the National Library. Oh look! All the paths are marked.'

143

'There's the Child's Garden,' said Gareth, pointing. 'See, there's another way up, from right back here. It comes out by where I left my bike.'

'Let's see what the article says.'

They pored over the map.

'I'm amazed nobody's tried to open the gardens up before now,' said Gareth. 'I mean, people must know about them.'

'The Historic Gardens people keep wanting to come here,' Alwena told him. 'They don't want other people tramping about because of destroying the what-do-you-call, the nature—'

'The ecology?'

'Yes, the ecology. And Dad's been too busy. He's always having to go to meetings and write reports.' She paused. 'And I've been ill. I've been ill almost all the time we've been here.'

'What'll happen if you don't get the Lottery money?'

'I don't know,' said Alwena.

'Might you have to leave?'

'I don't know.'

'I don't suppose you will,' said Gareth comfortingly. 'The University isn't going to let the place fall down, is it? And they'll have to have somebody to look after it.'

'I don't think that's the arrangement,' said Alwena, looking distressed. 'Dad's contract has got something in it about if they don't get the Lottery money.'

No wonder he was so twitchy, then, thought Gareth, who had been having the precariousness of employment drummed into him by his father pretty well non-stop these last few weeks.

'He likes it better like this, though,' said Alwena. 'With only us here. His great-grandfather worked here before the war. He was a steward, or something. His grandad used to tell Dad stories about it.'

'Llŷr's Nain worked here then as well,' said Gareth. 'The one who said there was no ghost. She was a servant.'

'It must have been hard work,' said Alwena. 'I wouldn't like to be somebody's servant.'

'She said there was always plenty of food at Plas Idaleg,' said Gareth.

'Before the war was ages ago,' said Alwena, counting decades backwards. 'Sixty years, easily. She must be very old.'

'People went out to work very young before the war, though.'

'I wonder if she remembers the gardens, or if they'd got overgrown by then?' Dad must know about this Nain, thought Alwena. And she must have known his grandfather.

She quite liked the idea of networks of people being connected with Plas Idaleg. Real people with families who'd done jobs, not just organisations and committees. But her father was funny about other people, he didn't seem to want them to come too close. She had assumed that this was because he was protecting her from insensitive strangers, but now she wondered if there might be other reasons as well.

She wished she could meet Llŷr's Nain and talk to her.

'Is Llŷr that boy who came with you that time? That tall boy?'

'That's him.'

If he comes again, I'll have to ask him about his Nain, she thought.

'Is he your friend?'

'I suppose so,' said Gareth. 'When he's not acting stupid.'

'Will he be coming here again?'

'I dunno. He might. He's not that bothered.' Gareth hoped not. He did not want Llŷr to come sailing in to be greeted by Alwena wanting to know all about his Nain. He was not interested in knowing about the people who had worked at the Plas. He wanted it to remain a lost, deserted mansion full of spaces and shadows and mysteries.

'I'd better go soon,' said Gareth, later that afternoon. 'I need to get my bike before it gets dark.'

'What if it's got a puncture? It's been there ages.'

'It ought to be all right. Nobody will have touched it, will they?'

'Only the Child, perhaps,' said Alwena.

'You've not been up to the Garden again, then.'

'Not in real life,' said Alwena. 'I keep dreaming about it, though.'

'I'll take you up there again one day, if you like,' said Gareth rashly. 'In the Christmas holidays, p'raps, if it's not too snowy.'

'Oh!' There was no mistaking the alarm that flashed across her face. 'Oh no, you mustn't trouble.'

'I won't let you fall off,' said Gareth. 'And I could carry you up, easy. We ought to see if we can find all the walks before the Historical people, don't you think?'

'Oh, yes, I'd like that.' Her face lit up again and he dropped his eyes shyly. Honest to God, if the others could see him now, having these long conversations about gardens with a disabled fifteen year old girl, they'd think he'd lost his marbles.

As they began to close the books and journals which littered the table Alwena's father came into the room, looking harrassed and angry.

'Where's your mother?' he demanded of Alwena.

'I think she's in the darkroom.'

'You shouldn't be in here, Alwena, it's too cold. We don't allow students in here without supervision,' he said to Gareth. 'What are you doing, anyway? What are all these books doing out? What's that map? Good God, I've been searching for this map—and what's this—' He picked up the copy of *Ceredigion* which was still open at the article about the Plas Idaleg gardens. He looked from the journal to the map. 'What are you doing?' he asked again. 'Is this the missing *Ceredigion*? Where did you find it? Where have you been poking about?'

Pushing Gareth roughly to one side he swept up the map from the table and began to fold it. Gareth thought with relief of the photocopy, safe in his bedroom at home.

'I borrowed it,' said Alwena loudly. 'I borrowed the map as well. I've had them in my bedroom.'

'No, I borrowed it,' said Gareth. 'I borrowed the map and the book. I brought them back today. I couldn't bring them back before, because of the fog.'

'No, it was me,' said Alwena. 'It was me, Daddy.'

Roscoe Morgan straightened up. He stepped up to

Gareth, forcing him to take a step back. 'I think you'd better leave,' he said. 'These are very important historical documents. How dare you remove them without my permission. Be quiet, Alwena.'

'But it was me—'

'Do as I say, Alwena, please. As for you—Lloyd, that's your name, isn't it?—please get your belongings and go. And don't let me see you here again. I shall be speaking to your Headmaster about this.'

Gareth's face burned with anger. He wanted to shout abuse at Roscoe Morgan. Bully! Bastard! He clenched his teeth over the words, then snatched up his parka and rucksack and walked out of the room.

Chapter Eleven

'Well, that's it,' said Alwena's father, still in a thunderous fury several hours later. 'She's not going to *that* school, if I have to educate her myself.'

Alwena's mother sighed. She looked exhausted.

'I don't know what you think you were doing, leaving them alone together. Anything could have happened.'

'Nothing happened,' said Alwena from her corner. 'We were only talking. We were looking at the map, that's all.' She must have said this a hundred times. She was trembling with the effort of not crying. Olwen pressed against her knees, looking anxiously up at Alwena from her small eyes.

'Alwena, I've told you to be quiet. I don't like this new, disobedient Alwena, this sly, deceitful Alwena.'

'For God's sake,' said Alwena's mother. 'This is the twentieth century.' She stood up. 'Alwena, perhaps you'd better go to bed. I'll bring you some supper on a tray.'

'I'll put her to bed,' said her father, also standing up. 'You get the food. We've got to get to the bottom of this.' He came towards Alwena and seized Olwen's collar to pull her out of the way.

For the first time in her life Alwena was afraid of her father. 'No,' she cried.

'Roscoe,' said Alwena's mother. 'Sit down. I'm beginning to think you must be unwell.' She took hold of his arm and pulled him away from Alwena, forcing him round to face her. 'Roscoe, if you don't sit down *this minute* I am going to put Alwena in the car and drive her over to my mother's.'

He snatched his arm away. Stepping backwards he kicked Olwen who recoiled, whimpering in distress. 'That's it!' he shouted. 'I've had enough. I'm going to see T. J. I'll give him A Level projects. If I hadn't let him talk me into letting him bring those great yobs here we wouldn't be having all this trouble. As if I haven't got enough on my plate!' He slammed out of the room. A few moments later they heard the outside door slam. Alwena's mother waited for a moment, then went to the telephone and dialled. She murmured a few words into the receiver before replacing it on the handset.

Alwena's tears got the better of her at last.

'Why is Dad so angry?' she sobbed. 'We weren't doing anything bad.'

'I know, love,' said her mother. 'It's not your fault. I think things are beginning to get on top of your father.'

'I don't want to get Gareth into trouble,' wept Alwena. 'I borrowed the book. I wanted to find out about the Child's Garden. I kept it a secret because you never talked about the Child.'

'Don't worry.' Alwena's mother pulled a chair up close to Alwena's and stroked her daughter's hair. 'Cheer up. Let's have some supper.'

'What about Dad?'

'If T. J.'s got any sense he'll take him to the pub and they'll get some food there,' said her mother. 'He'll be all right. He'll calm down once he's had a good moan to T. J.'

'He'll blame Gareth for everything. He won't let him come here any more.'

'T. J. won't let him do that, Alwena. He knows your father, and I daresay he knows Gareth well enough too.' Her mother sighed. 'I knew we should have made sure you had more friends of your own age.'

'Gareth is my friend,' said Alwena. 'He talks to me. We have proper conversations. And I'm not deceitful, Mum.' She began to cry again. Olwen crept across the carpet and put her head on Alwena's lap, which made her weep even harder.

'I know you're not deceitful, sweetheart,' said her mother. 'Anyway, we've all got the right to some privacy in our lives. But fathers don't always like it when their daughters start to grow up. Your Dad's a bit jealous of Gareth, you know.'

'*Jealous*?'

Alwena's mother smiled. 'Well, he's used to being the only man in your life! And now here's this handsome young Galahad riding across the hills through all weathers to see his daughter!'

'It's because he likes the *house*,' said Alwena, blushing scarlet. 'Not because he likes *me*.'

He went off yesterday without even saying goodbye, she thought, gazing down at Olwen's sad eyes. He didn't even look at me. He was so furious. I'll never see him again, she thought. Not even at school. And he'll never carry me up to the garden now.

'You seemed to be getting on pretty well,' her mother was saying. 'You obviously found plenty to talk about. Did you find the garden, between you?'

'We found it separately,' said Alwena sleepily. Then she realised what she'd said and went scarlet once more, this time with horror. 'I mean,' she added hurriedly, 'I had the article, and he had the map.'

Her mother frowned. She looked carefully at Alwena for a long moment. She's remembering the afternoon I got lost, Alwena thought desperately. She's going to ask me.

'How about a nice boiled egg for supper?' said her mother. 'I'm starving, I don't know about you.'

Alwena's heart rattled with relief. 'Can I have two eggs, please?' she said.

*   *   *

'And how was *she*?' Llŷr asked Gareth with a leer, in the boys' toilets at break the following Monday.

'Do you want another nose-bleed?'

'Not specially, thanks.' Llŷr grinned sideways at Gareth as they slouched along the corridor to the drinks machines.

'I've been banned,' said Gareth at last.

'What! But you weren't even out last Saturday night.'

'Not from the pub,' said Gareth. 'From Plas Idaleg.' He waited while the machine splashed water onto coffee granules in the polystyrene cup. Llŷr got himself a coke and they went into the school refectory where they were waved at by Elin and Gwenno.

'Go on, then,' said Llŷr as they sat down. 'Let's have the *hanes*. Tell us the story. Have you heard,' he said to the girls, 'Elin was right. Sleeping Beauty at Plas Idaleg.'

'Do you want your head knocked off—'

Elin looked furious. 'Oh, so that's why you've been slogging up there every weekend.'

'Shut up,' said Gareth. 'It's Roscoe Morgan's daughter, that's all. She's little. She's got arthritis or something. She walks with a stick.'

Gwenno said, 'I never knew that. She doesn't come to school, does she?'

'She's been ill. Before that she went to Aber.'

'So what were you doing to her, to get yourself banned?' asked Llŷr.

'Leave off, would you.'

'I don't suppose it would take much,' said Gwenno. 'He had that look about him, that Roscoe Morgan.'

Gareth relaxed, grateful for Gwenno's matter-of-fact tone. 'I'd borrowed this old map,' he said. 'He said I'd stolen it. I'd only borrowed it. I'd taken it back, I was showing it to Alwena. That's the girl.'

'Nice name,' said Llŷr.

'He played hell, he did,' said Gareth. 'Her father. You'd think I was—' he shrugged.

'What's she like?' asked Elin suspiciously.

'I dunno,' said Gareth. 'Little. Her hands are all bent in like this. She's got dark hair.'

'Poor thing,' said Gwenno. 'Stuck out in the hills in that great barn of a house with a father like that. Is he trying to hide her away or something? It's not fair, is it?'

Elin's jealous expression faded. Gareth watched her irritably. Elin was so stupid. At least Gwenno was sensible. None of them would understand the full story. They wouldn't understand why Alwena had climbed up to the garden. They wouldn't understand about the Child. They wouldn't understand—Gareth hardly knew himself what he was trying to express—the whole thing about the map, the climb, the prospect of the world—

Least of all would they understand why he felt worried about Alwena. Her father had virtually thrown him out of the house but he still felt guilty about walking out on her the way he did. He felt he had abandoned her. She needs to be got out, he thought.

Gwenno said, 'Those funny noises we heard—was it her?'

'The ghost!' said Elin.

'Does T. J. know you've been banned?' asked Llŷr. 'Are we all banned? What about your A Level project?'

'I dunno,' said Gareth. He felt very out on a limb this morning. He did not want to listen to his friends chewing over the Plas Idaleg saga. He did not want to talk to T. J. In his head, he was at Plas Idaleg fighting it

153

out with Roscoe Morgan, bloodying *his* nose while Alwena stood watching. Even that did not seem to resolve anything. It left an unpleasant taste in his mouth.

A double Maths period following break brought him some relief by forcing him to concentrate on matters far removed from lost maps and irate fathers. Gwenno, the only other one of his friends doing A Level Maths, sat next to him but made no further attempt to pump him about Alwena during the lesson. Her interest in Plas Idaleg was minimal. She didn't need it, thought Gareth, to feed her belief that there was something more to life than—well, just something *more*. She and her violin had already been to Germany and Holland with the National Youth Orchestra of Wales. Her future already contained Paris and New York, she didn't have to dream about them, they were just waiting for her. She didn't even dream about her music very much, it seemed to Gareth. She just did it.

As he was eating pie and chips, sitting with Llŷr, Gwenno and Elin at lunchtime, T. J. tapped him on the shoulder. Smoking was forbidden in school but T. J. still chewed his empty pipe.

'Can you come to the staff room for a minute when you've finished your dinner, please Gareth?'

'Sir,' mumbled Gareth, not looking up.

The four of them watched in silence as T. J. meandered away between the crowded tables, bending here and there to listen to a remark called out to him by one pupil or another.

We're all actors in his drama, thought Gareth. His history.

154

Claustrophobia gripped him. He was possessed by a longing to stand up, throw down his books, cast off his blazer and walk out of the school forever. He thought wildly of the Post Office Savings Account his mother insisted he kept; saw himself cashing it, hitching to Aberystwyth or Carmarthen to catch the London train.

'Don't look like that,' said Llŷr. 'He's not going to eat you.'

'He already has,' said Gareth. Gwenno laughed mockingly. The laugh of the free, he thought, staring at the food congealing on his plate. He pushed back his chair. 'Better go, I suppose.'

'Honest to God,' said Llŷr. 'What's he going to accuse you of, rape?'

Elin sniggered. Gareth glared at her and walked off without replying.

He knocked on the staff room door and was told that Mr Mostyn was outside smoking his pipe and had left instructions for Gareth to join him. The prospect of being marched round the playing field being ticked off by T. J. in front of the whole school did nothing for Gareth's mood, but he went resignedly off in search of him.

T. J. was watching a group of year nine boys half-heartedly running about after a football, shivering in their cotton shorts in the bleak, showery wind. They were being shouted at by the PE teacher who wore a thick black jogging suit. Which just about summed up, thought Gareth, why he hated all forms of outdoor sport except tennis.

'Ah, there you are,' said T. J., taking his pipe out of

his mouth and coughing hoarsely. 'Come across to the library with me, I want to do a little bit of research. I thought you could give me a bit of help. You've got a free period, haven't you?'

'Yes.' Gareth had in fact been planning to sneak off home out of the way, and cut Physics at the end of the afternoon. Ah, well, at least this way he wouldn't get a row from his mother.

The school library was attached to what was still described as the Sixth Form block. In the afternoons it operated as the town's branch library and was out of bounds to the whole school apart from the Sixth Form, which meant it was useful for quiet retreats or rendezvous. It stood next to a large, pink, detached house in which his father was installing a new central heating system. The van with *Bryn Lloyd, Plumber and Heating Engineer* painted on the side was parked on double yellow lines outside the house, its back doors open. Inevitably his father appeared just as they were crossing the road from the main school block.

'Afternoon there, T. J.' he bawled, reaching into the van and pulling out yards of copper piping. 'I hope you're managing to get more work out of him than I do!'

'Gareth's doing very well, Bryn, don't you worry,' replied T. J.

'Head in the clouds!' retorted Gareth's father.

'Well, there are interesting things to be found in clouds, sometimes,' said T. J. 'And someone's got to look for 'em.'

'Well, he is doing physics, I suppose.' Gareth's father gave a cackle of laughter and thumped his son between the shoulder blades with his free hand. 'Does he write up what he finds there, though, T. J., that's the question isn't it? Scientific enquiry!'

'Your father,' said T. J., smiling round his pipe as they pushed open the double doors into the library, 'doesn't change a bit. Sharp as a needle!'

Inside, T. J. exchanged a few words with the School Librarian, a new young man in a fashionably baggy suit and a dirty turquoise tie. From the guy's cautious nod Gareth deduced that this was someone else whose history T. J. had had a hand in.

The Reference and Local History section was housed in a small alcove by the library entrance. It was lined with reference books and journals, their back numbers bound in dull blues and greens. There was a brown set of Encyclopaedia Britannica and an unbound series of the University of Wales *Geiriadur Cymraeg*. In a corner bay was a set of identical volumes bound in red cloth at graduated stages of fading. *Ceredigion* was embossed in gold on their spines.

'Is that a full set?' asked Gareth indignantly.

'Yes, yes, of course it is,' replied T. J.

'The way that—Mr Morgan was going on about the one that was missing you'd think it was the only one in Wales!'

T. J. said, 'That still doesn't mean it was all right for you to take it, Gareth.'

Gareth began to say, 'I didn't!' then broke off. He closed his mouth.

'Unless of course it was Alwena who took it, not you,' continued T. J. 'You could have come here at any time and looked up what you needed to. There was no need for you to pinch an odd volume.'

Gareth said nothing.

'I always thought it was a bit unlikely, anyway,' said T. J., watching Gareth out of his shrewd old eyes.

'That Roscoe Morgan's a nutcase,' said Gareth. 'I wasn't doing anything. I was just talking to his daughter. We were looking at a map.'

'Ah, yes, the map. An old map of the estate, is that right?'

I don't see why I should tell him, thought Gareth angrily. It's nothing to do with him what we were looking at.

'I bet there are other maps as well,' he said. 'There must be maps, they must have needed one when they put in for the Lottery money. I don't know what I've done wrong. I'm supposed to be writing about the Plas for my A Levels. I've got to do research about it. Why shouldn't I look at a map? What's the big secret?'

'There are no big secrets, Gareth,' said T. J. 'You can find all the facts about the history of Plas Idaleg,' he paused, then added, 'and the people who have lived there, from articles in these journals, if you use the indexes. Maps too.'

Gareth threw himself into a chair. 'So what you're saying is, I can't go to Plas Idaleg any more, but I can carry on doing my project here.'

'I'm sorry in my heart this has happened, Gareth,' said T. J.

'He's a right nutter! We weren't doing anything!' Gareth repeated. 'I feel right sorry for that girl stuck

158

there with him for a father. What's the matter with him? Why doesn't he just put barbed wire all round the place and be done with it?'

'Alwena's father,' said T. J. reflectively, 'he's a very complex man. Got a lot on his plate at the moment, too.'

Gareth nearly said, 'Big deal,' but stopped himself. He tilted his chair back and tried to show how boring he found Alwena's father.

'If you think a bit more about the history of the Plas,' said T. J., 'and if you do a bit more reading, you might understand things a bit better. Give you some real insights into your project too, I shouldn't wonder. But you won't understand anything if you stay in a temper, Gareth. A bit of objectivity, a bit of maturity, is what's needed.'

He sucked his pipe thoughtfully, took it out of his mouth and looked into the bowl.

'I'm not preaching you a sermon,' he said with a smile. 'Though I daresay you think I am.'

He's talking in riddles, thought Gareth. Then he thought, he's trying to get me to come out with why Alwena was looking at the map.

Did T. J. know about the garden? He must do, it was all written down somewhere. Anyway, T. J. knew everything. He was like a one-man CIA.

He doesn't know we've found the garden yet though, he thought. He doesn't know we've been there. But he knows there's something.

T. J. watched him for a while. He never seemed to be in any hurry. Presently he said, 'A useful thing might be for you to look in the old church. It's quite interesting

159

inside. There's been a lot of damage done there over the years but it's still pretty much as Edward Jones-Mortimer built it. It might explain a few things to you.'

He put his pipe back into his mouth and pulled out his pocket watch. 'Time we were getting back. I've got my Year Sevens in ten minutes and they need licking into shape.'

But what about Alwena? Gareth found himself wanting to ask. What's going to happen to her? He did not dare say a word. It was as though he would be betraying her.

Don't be stupid, he told himself. You don't know what you're talking about.

He stood up wearily and followed T. J. outside.

Chapter Twelve

'It's my fault,' said Alwena's father for the hundredth time, coming out of his office and sitting opposite Alwena at her work table in the Octagon Library. 'I know I've been neglecting you. You're alone here so much, and I'm so busy with all these meetings.'

Alwena was beginning to find her father's remorse even more upsetting than his anger. She dreaded being on her own with him, because he would immediately find an excuse to begin all over again. Mid mornings, when her mother went to make coffee, were the ideal opportunity. It had been three days now, at least.

'I'll try to spend more time with you in the future. The University will have to understand. When I think what you said to me only a few weeks ago, how much you love being here with me and Mummy in the peace and quiet. It pricks my conscience terribly that I can't be here for you more.'

Did I say that? thought Alwena, doodling in the margins of her exercise book. I suppose I must have done. Why did I say that? Was it true?

'I've been so looking forward to the time when we can explore the estate together. There's so much to discover, but I want you to get really well first. The grounds are so overgrown and dangerous. Alwena, please, listen to me.'

Alwena looked over her shoulder towards the library door, longing for her mother to appear with the tray. The rain rattled against the glass of the lantern high above her.

'When the Spring comes, we'll have more time. You'll be stronger. We'll explore then, I promise. We'll get the maps out and see if we can't find some of Sir Edward's old gardens. Alwena, what do you think about that?'

'That will be nice,' said Alwena politely. Her heart was heavy as she spoke, as though she were telling a terrible untruth. She could not look at her father.

'And perhaps in the Spring, you'll be well enough to start riding properly again,' said her father. 'If the physiotherapist thinks you're ready for it. We might even start looking for a nice, quiet pony. You'd like that, wouldn't you?'

Alwena's eyes started up to meet her father's. He was

gazing at her eagerly. 'I know it's what you've missed most, riding,' he said. 'You've never mentioned it, but I think I'm right, aren't I?'

Alwena could not think what to say. She took a deep breath, then released it with relief when she heard her mother's footsteps approaching along the passage.

'Thank you very much, Daddy,' she whispered.

'That's my Alwena,' said her father. He smiled up at his wife as she came into the library. 'I've told Alwena we might think about getting her a pony in the Spring.'

'What a good idea,' said her mother, putting down the tray of coffee mugs. 'It'll give her a bit more independence.' She smiled drily at her husband who said at once, 'I know you think I want to keep Alwena a child forever, but it's not true!'

'No, dear, of course not,' said Alwena's mother, handing him his coffee.

Alwena watched her parents fight a short, silent battle of wills as her father's temper flared in his face and her mother faced him coolly. She wanted to weep with misery. How long was this drear, drear life to go on? Was it really her own fault, for letting her father spoil her all these months and years, for being his good little daughter? Had she really believed that all she wanted was to stay here at Plas Idaleg with her mother and father *and nobody else* for ever and ever?

She must have felt like that. She had hated those Sixth Formers that first time. She had hated their loud, tall cheerfulness, the way they joked and teased each other. Well, she'd got what she wanted. They'd gone away and they wouldn't be coming back now.

Do you remember how they laughed? she asked the Child in her head. You could hear them laughing all through the house. I was so furious!

Well, the girls were horrible, she thought. They never stopped moaning about the cold. She didn't mind if she never saw them again. Gareth, though, he was different.

Her parents were being ridiculously careful not to mention Gareth's name in her presence. It was as though they both wanted her to forget he ever existed. They couldn't stop her thinking about him, though. In her imagination her cheek still lay against his shoulder, his fair hair tickling her face, as he carried her down from the Child's garden. She could still see his broad grin, feel the grasp of his strong hand on her elbow as he pulled her to her feet at the end of her precipitous ride on Bedwyr. They had long debates in her head, about the lost gardens and the Child and why Sir Vernon Roderick was called the Wickedest Man in Wales.

It was terrible to think that she might never have a proper conversation with him ever again. Or with anyone else, come to that. Except T. J., and perhaps one day all those archaeologists who were supposed to be coming, and even then it would be all about how wonderfully clever she was despite being so disabled. Her whole life was going to be like that. The only thing she would be famous for, the only thing anyone would ever want to talk about, would be her illness.

It must have been like that for the Child.

I told you, said the Child, in her head. We could have flown. You didn't want to fly.

Alwena's nightmare still haunted her. It was as though

the Child was mocking her. We could have flown, but *you* didn't want to.

The terror of that fall, over and over, mile after mile, the forest waiting to engulf her.

Alwena's stomach turned over.

We'll have to fly at some point, said the Child impatiently. Whether you want to or not.

'Have a biscuit, Alwena,' said her mother. 'Whatever are you dreaming about? You look quite faraway.'

'She's thinking about the pony,' said her father. 'I knew she'd be pleased.'

*   *   *

The following day, Thursday, Alwena was still in bed when she heard her father leave the house for a nine o'clock meeting at the University in Aberystwyth. The back door slammed rather loudly, making Olwen bark, and Alwena guesed that her parents had been arguing again. She could not help feeling relieved at the prospect of a morning without her father.

When she came downstairs for breakfast she was surprised to see that the family car was still parked in the yard outside the kitchen window.

'It's worked out very well,' said her mother. 'T. J.'s on this particular committee as well so they've gone together. That means we can have the car. I fancy a day out, Alwena, don't you?'

There was something about her mother's tone that made Alwena want to ask, does Dad know? Then it occurred to her that this would explain the argument.

'It's your father's birthday next week. I thought we

could go to the Craft Centre in Abercoed and see if we can find him a nice sweater or something. Or we could try Aberaeron, or Lampeter p'raps.'

Abercoed! thought Alwena.

The High School in Abercoed was right on the main road. If they went to Lampeter, they'd have to drive past it. And if they were driving past it at dinner time, they might, they just might see Gareth.

'Is it all right to leave the Plas without anybody here?' she asked, stop herself agreeing too eagerly.

'Of course it is,' said her mother briskly. 'That's why we have locks on the doors. Not that there's anything to steal, even if we didn't.'

So there had been a row. Well, it would be for a good cause if they were buying Dad a birthday present. He wouldn't be able to be angry about that.

'What about Olwen?'

'She can come with us. We'll take her for a walk on the beach. Come and have your breakfast, Alwena. How are you feeling today?'

'Fine,' said Alwena, surprising herself. She realised that she had got out of bed, bathed and dressed almost without noticing whether today was a good or a bad day. 'Fine,' she repeated, smiling at her mother.

'Good! You're really coming on now, aren't you? We'll be able to show the doctor some real progress next time we see him.'

Alwena sat down at the breakfast table and poured herself some cornflakes. She ate a couple of mouthfuls, then put down her spoon and said, 'Mum, I want to see the doctor on my own next time.'

She had not realised she was going to say this until she had said it. She looked uncertainly at her mother's face, waiting for her reaction.

Her mother brought two glasses of orange juice to the table, put one down by Alwena's plate then sat down to drink the other herself.

'I don't see why not,' she said at last. 'You're growing up now, Alwena.'

'What do you think Dad will say?'

'I'll talk to your father. You wouldn't mind if we came in at the end, perhaps, if there was anything the doctor needed us all to know?'

'Oh no, it's just—' Alwena broke off, losing her nerve.

'You don't have to explain,' said her mother gently. 'But Daddy might find it a bit hard to accept at first, you know that, don't you? Better not say anything until nearer the time. Your appointment's not for ages yet.'

'All right.' Alwena smiled gratefully at her mother.

An hour later they were driving away from Plas Idaleg, with Olwen straining excitedly to look out of the window from behind the grid that kept her penned in the rear of the hatchback. Alwena watched the house recede in the wing mirror, a vast mass of shapes with the weak morning sun behind it.

Alwena's mother said sadly, 'The place gets to one, doesn't it?'

'Oh yes.'

They both sighed. Alwena hovered on the edge of telling her mother about the Child, and the garden, and the dream, but could not quite do it.

'Shall we always live there?' she asked suddenly.

Her mother braked as they reached the end of the drive, then pulled carefully out onto the road and turned south over the old stone bridge.

'I suppose,' she said eventually, 'the University will always need a Warden of some kind to look after the place, even if the Lottery bid doesn't come off.'

'Might it not come off?'

'There are a lot of problems. There's quite a lot of opposition to the project, because of the cost for one thing. But the Plas is a listed building, so it can't just be allowed to fall down.'

'Dad wouldn't mind if it wasn't restored,' said Alwena. 'As long as we could stay there. He'd prefer it.'

'Your Dad would have armed sentries on the gates if it were up to him,' said her mother tartly.

Alwena could not think of a reply to this which would not make her sound disloyal to her father.

'Sorry,' said her mother. 'Forget I said that. But it would be nice to have a bit more life about the place, wouldn't it? I shall be glad when David comes home for Christmas.'

'Mm,' said Alwena. 'David's so noisy.'

'Probably good for us,' said her mother with a laugh.

Abercoed was a small town clustered tightly around a crossroads. Turning left at the junction they drove into a small square with an inn on one side and a statue of a man in a Victorian frock coat in the middle. Alwena's mother found a parking space in the square near the *Craft Centre* and they got out of the car, leaving Olwen gazing sorrowfully at them out of the rear window.

Alwena and her mother enjoyed pottering around in the Craft Centre. They chose a thick sweater in tobacco brown wool for her father's birthday present, and Alwena bought a pair of gloves for David for Christmas.

'We ought to take Olwen out for a quick run,' said Alwena's mother as they returned to the car after an early lunch of soup and sandwiches at the cafe by the crossroads. 'But we'd better get out of town a bit first.'

Alwena held her breath as they drove back towards the junction. When they turned left for Lampeter instead of carrying straight on for Aberaeron her heart began to thump anxiously. She must not miss a single second of the drive past the school.

'I tell you what,' said her mother. 'Let's stop here and take her for a quick run down by the school playing field.'

She was already pulling into the kerb outside a low, grey building that had a notice saying Sixth Form Block fixed to the wall. The sight of it made Alwena's legs feel quite weak. In the back of the car Olwen began to bark, her tail quivering with excitement.

There were quite a few people in school uniform coming and going between this block and the main school building on the opposite side of the road, but nobody tall enough to be Gareth.

'It's their dinner break, by the looks of things,' said Mrs Morgan.

Alwena began to lose her nerve. 'P'raps we'd better not take Olwen out just here. She might get over-excited and bite somebody.'

'A quick walk on the lead won't hurt. We'll just go

down the lane a little way.' Mrs Morgan was already getting out of the car and coming round to the passenger side to let Alwena out.

'Okay? Here's your stick.'

'No! I can manage! I don't want it!'

She was definitely not going to be seen walking with a stick with all these people about to stare at her.

'All right,' said her mother. 'If you're sure. I'll just let Olwen out.'

Olwen leapt to the ground, barking joyfully and dragging on the lead so that Mrs Morgan staggered.

'Come on, let's cross the road quickly. Hold on to my arm, Alwena.' Alwena hesitated on the kerb, looking up and down the road. A transit van slowed for them to cross safely, and Mrs Morgan gave the driver a grateful nod.

A narrow lane led between the main school buildings and the playing field, on the gate to which was a sign saying, 'Abercoed High School: No Dogs.'

'Dash,' said Mrs Morgan. 'I'd forgotten. Never mind, we'll just go down the lane a bit. Are you okay?'

'Yes, thank you.'

'This school's different from Aberystwyth, isn't it? It's nearly all on one level. And much smaller, of course.'

Alwena thought, Mum's brought me here on purpose. I should have realised.

A month ago she would have had a tantrum about it.

As they walked back up the lane, taking their time so that Olwen could sniff at every inch of the hedgerow, she watched as dozens of people from eleven to eighteen dawdled or marched or ran in and out of the school buildings. There was even a boy in a wheelchair, wheeling himself along energetically and talking hard to another couple of boys. No one paid any attention to Alwena, until suddenly Olwen began to strain at the lead, barking and wagging her tail.

Gareth had crossed the road from the Sixth Form Block, and she had been so absorbed in watching the wheelchair boy that she hadn't even noticed.

*   *   *

There was no mistaking that bark. Gareth hung back behind Llŷr and the girls to make sure, but it was indeed the Child's bull terrier. He still thought of Alwena as the Child. She was there herself too, and that was the mother.

He had to fight off the impulse to dive back into the Sixth Form Block, in case the father was about.

He gave them a quick nod and smile and would have continued on his way, but Gwenno was already saying, 'Oh look! I love bull terriers!' and bending down to make friends with the dog.

'They've got such sad faces,' said Gwenno to Alwena. 'Is she yours?'

Alwena nodded, her eyes on the ground.

'Hello, Gareth,' said the Child's mother. 'How are you?'

'Fine, thanks,' muttered Gareth. The paralysis in his mind relaxed and he remembered her name. 'Fine, thanks, Mrs Morgan.' He crouched down by Olwen who began to lick his face avidly. Behind him, Llŷr and Elin

170

stared blatantly at Alwena. He wished he were ten miles away.

'You're the girl who lives at Plas Idaleg,' Gwenno was saying to Alwena in her usual direct way. 'We thought you were a ghost! And the dog too! What's her name?'

'Olwen,' said Alwena. She had taken her mother's hand and was leaning against her for support. Gareth noticed she was not carrying her stick.

'Oh, that's a really good name. She looks like an Olwen.'

As Gareth straightened up he caught Alwena's eye. She smiled quickly and looked away. His conscience jabbed at him for some reason.

'Well! Gaynor!'

Claire Davies the Art teacher was coming towards them, a pile of books in her arms. She and Alwena's mother greeted each other with delight, and they fell into a well-I-never, how-long-has-it-been kind of conversation. Gareth said, 'Bye, Alwena,' with relief, and followed the others in the direction of the refectory. Looking over his shoulder he saw the two women and Alwena crossing the road towards the library.

'So that's her!' said Elin as they queued for food. 'Did you see her hands? Poor little kid!'

'I'll say,' said Gwenno. 'Especially if she's Roscoe the Terrible's daughter. That's a worse handicap than arthritis in my book.'

Gareth thought, I hope he hasn't been giving her a hard time about the map. I bet he has.

He tried to think, oh well, it can't be helped, but it didn't work. The need to do something nagged at him.

He began on his burger and chips, silently listening to the others discussing Alwena and the dog and her awful father. Pushing his food away half-eaten he said, 'See you in a bit,' and hurried away before they could start asking questions.

Their car was still parked outside the library. Gareth knew it was the Morgans' because Olwen was penned in the back, gazing yearningly out of the window. He dashed across the road before she noticed him and went into the library. Alwena's mother and Claire Davies were sitting on the table in the Reference corner, deep in a conversation punctuated with groans and bursts of laughter. He slid past into the Lending section, ignoring the suspicious look on the face of the new librarian.

Alwena was sitting in a chair in the corner by the children's books, awkwardly turning over the pages of a paperback. She started nervously at the sight of Gareth and the book fell to the floor.

Gareth bent to pick it up for her. Now he was here he could think of nothing to say. He wasn't very good at talking to girls at the best of times. He distrusted their habit of storing up your words and using them for strange manipulative purposes of their own. Llŷr said sisters were just as bad. Gwenno's directness was the exception that proved the rule but then so was every aspect of Gwenno. Funny how she and Elin were such big mates.

'Did you get a big row off your Dad?' Gareth asked Alwena, surprising himself by speaking while still thinking of Gwenno and Elin.

'Oh no—well, a bit,' said Alwena. She had gone red

172

and was looking down at her hands, curving them in towards herself as though trying to make them look smaller.

'I hope you told him it was my fault,' he said. 'I took the map.'

'I took the magazine,' whispered Alwena.

'It's not rare,' said Gareth. 'They've got a full set here. T. J. showed me. There's lots of articles about the Plas, I've been looking them up.'

She said nothing. Gareth noticed that she was gently pressing the knuckles of one hand with the fingers of the other. He had seen her do this before. 'Do your hands hurt you all the time?' he asked suddenly.

She shook her head and said something inaudible. Then she cleared her throat and said, 'They still swell up sometimes.' She stopped pressing her knuckles and folded her hands under her arms.

'Sorry,' said Gareth. 'I didn't mean to be rude.'

Alwena shook her head even harder. 'No, no, it's all right.' But her dark eyes, huge in her thin, pointed face, gazed at him desperately. Gareth, who had suffered the crushes of younger girls before, felt a twinge of anxiety. He shifted from one foot to the other and eyed the door.

'The other journals,' said Alwena. 'The ones you looked up. Did they say what happened to the Child?'

'The family left,' said Gareth. 'T. J. said.'

'Yes, I know. But what about after that?'

Gareth shook his head. 'No idea. He didn't say.'

'I keep dreaming about her,' said Alwena quickly, as though it was something to be ashamed of.

'Does your Mum know?'

'I don't know.'

'T. J. says I should go to that church,' said Gareth. 'He says there's a lot of stuff there about the family. Have you been there?'

'No.'

'That man built it, the one who built the Plas. The Child's father. I thought I might ride over and look at it next Saturday afternoon. T. J. says they usually leave it open.'

'Oh!' She looked scared. After a minute she said, 'Don't let Dad find out. He—' She sighed, and her voice faded away. Then she added more firmly, 'He can't mind, if T. J. suggested it. Anyway churches are for everybody.'

'We're chapel, actually,' said Gareth, and was pleased to see her giggle faintly. Then she said, in a struggling sort of voice, 'I'm sorry—I'm sorry Dad was so mad at you. He gets so tired, you see—and he worries about me too much—'

'It doesn't matter—'

Just then Alwena's mother's face appeared over the book stack. 'We'd better go, Alwena, or we'll never get to the beach. Claire and I haven't seen each other for years. We were at Swansea together. Hello again, Gareth.'

'I'm just getting a book,' he replied quickly, although Alwena's mother did not seem to be against him speaking to Alwena like her father was. 'See you,' he said to Alwena. As he escaped he was conscious of her eyes following him. Their anxious, yearning expression reminded him of the dog Olwen. It made him feel guiltier than ever.

Chapter Thirteen

'I bet you still haven't written any of them letters,' said Gareth's father, coming into the kitchen with oil on his hands as Gareth made himself tea in a mug on Saturday morning.

'I'm going to do it tomorrow,' he said, rubbing the sleep from his eyes with one hand and fishing the tea bag out of the mug with the other.

'I saw that chap from Bennett Evans Associates in Cardigan yesterday. He said if you write to him they might give you an interview.'

'What d'you mean, an interview?'

'I'm only telling you what he said. You think yourself lucky they owe me a favour about some building specs they lost. If they just give you the once-over and tell you you're wasting your time it'll be a step forward as far as I'm concerned. But it's up to you, boy.'

'Okay,' said Gareth.

'Thanks, Dad, for putting yourself out on my account,' said his father. 'Don't mention it, son. Anything I can do to help you make a future for yourself. Give me strength!'

'Thanks, Dad,' said Gareth. 'I mean, sorry. Thanks, Dad.' He spooned sugar into his tea and stirred it violently to avoid looking at his father.

'Give me strength!' repeated his father, digging his fingers into the tin of Swarfega by the sink and rubbing it over his hands and wrists. 'If I didn't know you better I'd think you were on something.'

'I'm not on anything.'

'No,' said his father. 'And if I thought you were, there'd be trouble.'

The band of steel round Gareth's head tightened beyond endurance. He banged his mug down on the table. 'Leave me alone, Dad, can't you? It's like living in a flaming cage round here!'

'The only cage is inside your head!' retorted his father. 'Now are you helping me today or are you off to that damned Plas again?'

'I'm meeting Llŷr,' said Gareth, calming down. 'We've got to finish this history project before the end of term. We're not going to the Plas. Only to this church. T. J. says—'

'All right, all right, spare me what T. J. says.'

'I'll help you tomorrow.'

'You'd better write that letter today then.'

'Okay.' It would be quite interesting, Gareth conceded to himself, to see the inside of an architect's office, if nothing else.

An hour later he wheeled his bicycle out of the garage and propped it against the house wall next to where his father was tidying up inside the back of his van. As he was pumping up the tyres a car drew up in the road at the end of their drive.

'Gareth! Hi, Gareth!'

He stood upright and turned to see Elin and Gwenno waving at him from the front of a pale blue Golf with rusty sills. Gwenno was in the driving seat, and he remembered her boasting that she had passed her driving test at half term.

'Hello, what's this?' said Gareth's father. 'I didn't

know you were seventeen, Gwenno. Will it be safe for us to venture out on the roads now, do you reckon?'

'That's not fair, Mr Lloyd, Gwenno's a very good driver,' said Elin, getting out of the car. 'She passed first time.'

'You girls,' said Gareth's father, looking with approval at Elin's short skirt and long legs, 'you've got more go in you than the boys these days.'

'Where are you going?' asked Gareth, ignoring his father.

'We're off to Plas Idaleg,' said Gwenno. 'You may be banned, but we're not. T. J. got us clearance.'

'Banned?' said Gareth's father, jerking round to face Gareth so abruptly that he banged his head on the van roof. 'What's this, Gareth? Who's banned you?'

'Don't worry, Mr Lloyd,' said Gwenno. 'He hasn't done anything wrong. Roscoe Morgan's a funny fellow.'

'I remember who he was, now,' said Gareth's father, rubbing his head. 'He's a son for Gruffydd Morgan the estate agent. I remember him from school. Nasty temper. What did you do to upset him, Gareth?'

Gareth didn't want to say, he thought I was getting too friendly with his daughter, not in front of Elin and Gwenno. 'It was all those awkward questions you wanted me to ask,' he said.

His father grinned. 'Oh aye,' he said. 'So he doesn't always go round half asleep then, girls.'

'Well,' said Elin.

'Most of the time,' said Gwenno.

Gareth glowered at them.

'We heard you were meeting Llŷr,' said Gwenno. 'We came to see if you wanted a lift.'

'Thanks,' said Gareth, 'but I've got stuff to do here first.'

'Are you coming to the Angel tonight?'

Gareth remembered that there had been some mention of a good band appearing at one of the pubs in Aberystwyth that evening. He looked sideways at his father. 'I ought to get back,' he said.

'You go to Aber if you want,' said his father. 'The girls'll bring you home safe and sound, I dare say.'

'Don't if you don't want to!' said Elin sharply.

'Okay,' said Gareth. But to avoid being stuck with them all day he added, 'Don't wait now, though. I'll see you up at Llŷr's.'

Elin began to frown, but Gwenno nudged her in the ribs and said, 'All right, Mister Independent. Cycle ten miles in the freezing cold if you must. Come on, Elin. 'Bye, Mr Lloyd.'

'Cheerio, girls,' said his father, winking at them. 'Drive carefully!' He made a great fuss of guiding Gwenno as she did a three-point turn in the estate road. Gareth watched the girls drive off, hoping Gwenno would stall the Golf at the junction, but she did not.

'Nice girls!' said his father. 'You're playing harder to get with them than I would, Gareth, I'll give you that.' He laughed suddenly, and slapped his son on the back. 'So Roscoe Morgan has banned you, has he? Boy, there's hope for you yet!'

*   *   *

Llŷr's Nain did not appear to have moved one inch from her seat in the inglenook since Gareth's last visit to the farm. She did not even come to the table for her mid-day dinner; instead a plate of boiled ham and parsley sauce and fingers of bread-and-butter was carried over to her and set on a tray which was laid across the arms of her chair. A cup of tea into which Llŷr's mother had poured a tot of rum was set down next to her plate, together with three digestive biscuits on a saucer.

'I used to cure the hams at the Plas,' she told Gareth. 'That was my job, after the pig killing. And making the brawn from the pig's head. The cook, she was from London, she would never do it.'

She was much more lucid today than she had been last time. It must be the rum, thought Gareth.

'Pheasants too,' she continued, lifting a forkful of ham unsteadily to her mouth. Sauce dripped on her chin. 'They used to hang them up for a fortnight.'

'Nain, not while we're eating our dinner,' groaned Llŷr's elder brother Rhys.

'Until the maggots had dropped off,' said Nain. 'Then it'd be my job to pluck 'em.'

'Nain!'

'Always plenty of food at Plas Idaleg,' mumbled Nain, slurping her tea.

'You'd think we starved ourselves here, in comparison,' said Llŷr's father cheerfully. 'The golden age, eh, Mam?' he roared at the old woman.

'The old gentleman was always very fair,' she said. 'Not like that old Major Morgan. He was a bully, he was.'

'The agent,' said Llŷr's father. 'I don't remember him. My Dad used to say he was a mean old so-and-so. It was him stopped the big dinners the family always used to

179

put on for the tenants, rent day. Said the estate couldn't carry it any longer. I remember his son, though—Roscoe Morgan's grandfather, that would be. Went in for an estate agency. I believe he tried to buy the Plas after the war. The old gentleman had died by then, of course.'

'Those Morgans always did fancy themselves,' said Llŷr's mother. '*Boneddigion*—gentry—I don't know what!'

'So that's why Roscoe Morgan's got himself back in there,' said Llŷr. 'Nowhere else grand enough. No wonder he can't stand us lot going there.'

Gareth said nothing. He was surprised to realise that he felt uncomfortable with this explanation of Roscoe Morgan's motives. For some reason it did not ring true. You could tell he felt passionately about the place, but surely it wasn't just because he wanted to be the Squire and not the agent—or warden, or whatever his job was called now. He looked up and saw that Nain was watching him as she munched her boiled ham.

'Always been Morgans at Plas Idaleg,' she said. 'Ever since Sir Vernon's time.'

He frowned, not sure if he had heard her correctly.

'What's in this church we're supposed to be looking at?' asked Llŷr, ignoring his grandmother.

'You don't have to come if you don't want to,' said Gareth.

'Oh, I don't mind. Anyway it's my A Level project as well, isn't it?'

'There was a fire there in the thirties,' said Llŷr's father. 'The inside is all rebuilt. They say there's the remains of an old statue, but that's about all.'

180

'Who's the statue of?'

'That family,' said Llŷr's father vaguely. 'The one with the daughter. Long time ago now. I've never seen it. Mam used to have to go to church there, of course, but our family's always been chapel. You used to have to go to that church, Mam, didn't you?' he shouted at his mother, but she was bending over her plate to catch the next mouthful of ham and didn't hear him.

'Come on,' said Llŷr to Gareth, finishing his food quickly and jumping up from the table. 'She won't tell us anything else now. Let's get down there and see for ourselves.'

*   *   *

'I think it's wonderful here, Mr Morgan,' said Gwenno, gazing earnestly at Alwena's father across the table in the Octagon Library. 'There's so much space. You've really got room to breathe. You could have fantastic open air concerts in the park.'

Alwena had helped her mother carry in a tray of coffee for the helpers at eleven o'clock, and had somehow found herself sitting down with them. She was beginning to be able to tell them apart now: Gwenno was the one who had admired Olwen, and Elin was the girl who had grumbled about the cold on their first visit to the Plas, and kept finding excuses to snuggle up to Gareth.

'Gwenno plays in the National Youth Orchestra for Wales,' Alwena's mother told her father, who was clutching his coffee mug as though for support. Alwena watched her mother sit down next to her father and put her hand on his knee as though for reassurance.

181

There had been a very unpleasant article in that morning's *Western Mail*, attacking the plans for Plas Idaleg, sneering at the claim that it was a place of unique historical importance and suggesting that the University would be better off developing it as a theme park. Her father had been wandering about in a state of panic all morning, thinking up one plan after another for responding to the article. Even telephone calls from T. J. and the Chairman of the Plas Idaleg Trust had failed to calm him down. When the two Ysgol Abercoed girls arrived he greeted them with a surly grunt and shut himself in his office, only reappearing when Alwena and her mother arrived with the coffee.

'Mam showed me that article in the paper this morning, Mr Morgan,' said Gwenno. 'Look at this, she said, just because they think we might be getting something in Mid Wales and not Cardiff for a change. Doesn't it make you sick?'

She's chatting him up! thought Alwena. She was impressed to see her father's face relax. His eyes focused on Gwenno as though noticing her for the first time.

'What instrument do you play?' he asked.

'Violin,' said Gwenno. 'A bit of harp, but the violin, mainly.'

'What about you, er—Elin?'

'Oh, I'm not artistic,' said Elin. 'Gwenno says I'm tone deaf. I'm going to be a physiotherapist.' Alwena did not miss Gwenno's astonished look. 'Yes I am, Gwenno,' said Elin. 'I told you.'

'Well blow me down!' said Gwenno.

182

'I have a physiotherapist,' said Alwena, because Elin was looking put out. 'Her name's Pam.'

'Oh yes,' said Elin. 'She was my physio when I broke my leg hurdling. She's good, isn't she?'

Alwena nodded, and ate a biscuit to overcome her shyness.

Gwenno said, 'You must have to have a lot of physio. I think you're terribly brave. She's terribly brave, isn't she, Mr Morgan?'

Alwena's father smiled for the first time that morning. He reached across the table and laid his hand over Alwena's. 'Oh yes,' he replied. 'Perhaps we don't tell her often enough how brave she is. Most people only have to be brave now and again, but Alwena has to be brave every day of her life.'

'I'm not,' said Alwena, mortified. 'I'm not a bit brave really.'

'Shall you be coming to our school?' asked Gwenno.

Alwena dared not look at her father. She did not know whether her mother had told him about their visit to the school the other day. 'I do my lessons here,' she said. 'I might be having a tutor.'

'What, in this room?' Elin tilted her chair and looked up at the lantern window. 'Our classrooms would be a bit of a come-down after these glass domes and marble pillars, I can tell you.'

'We're wondering what to do,' said Alwena's mother, glancing at her husband. 'Alwena will be fifteen next year. GCSE year.'

'Same as my sister Bethan,' said Gwenno. 'Gosh, she's a pain, Mrs Morgan. Horse mad, she is.'

'Alwena used to ride a lot, before she fell ill,' said Alwena's mother. 'And you hope to start again soon, don't you, Alwena? Pam's all for it.'

'We're thinking of looking out for a pony in the spring,' said her father.

Alwena took a deep breath, looking from her mother to her father, then Gwenno to Elin. It was astonishing to hear her father being so pleasant to two girls he hardly knew.

It must be because the boys aren't here, she thought. Gareth and that other one. Llŷr. The boys wind him up, but the girls chat him up. She stifled a little laugh.

Where was Gareth, anyway? Had he been to the church yet? Saturday afternoon, he'd said. What time was it now? How was she going to get to the church?

'Is that your donkey outside?' Gwenno was asking her. 'He's sweet, isn't he? You've got some nice pets.'

'Bedwyr,' said Mrs Morgan, 'is not sweet. He's a stubborn, idle old gent.'

Alwena said loyally, 'He's all right, really.' He'd brought her safely down from the garden, after all.

Her mother said, 'You generally ride him for a bit in the afternoon, don't you, Alwena? Not on her own yet, though,' she added to Elin and Gwenno. 'Bedwyr wouldn't move a step if someone didn't lead him.'

'Push him, you mean,' said Alwena's father, pulling a face.

'I'll tell you what,' said Gwenno. 'We'll take you out on him this afternoon, Alwena. Elin'll push and I'll pull.'

They all laughed. 'That's very kind of you both,' said

Alwena's mother. 'You'd rather do that than come shopping in Aber with me, wouldn't you, Alwena?'

They could take me to the church, thought Alwena, shaken by this sudden solution to her problem.

No, no, she had to be on her own.

She'd never get there any other way.

She'd have to tell them why she wanted to go there. No no, it wasn't possible, she had to be on her own.

'Alwena?' said her mother. 'She's come over all shy,' she said to Elin and Gwenno. 'It's a long time since she's had any friends to talk to.'

*   *   *

'Which way shall we go?' asked Elin, leading Bedwyr with Alwena on board under the stable yard arch. 'You know the best walks round here.'

'Not really,' said Alwena, wriggling her feet in the stirrup irons so she could sit in the saddle as though she was riding properly, not just sitting on Bedwyr's back. 'There are a lot of paths, but they're all so overgrown.'

'See, it's us rescuing the Sleeping Beauty from the hundred year old spell,' Gwenno said to Elin. 'Not those old boys. Don't you feel a bit like that sometimes?' she asked Alwena. 'I mean, I know you've got all this room, but it's an awful lonely sort of place, isn't it?'

Alwena shook her head. She had to stop herself saying, *I* don't feel like that, not a bit, but the Child did. Does.

The Child was still under the spell. A two hundred year old spell.

'When I'm better, I'll be able to explore more,' she said.

185

'They ought to turn these woods into a nature reserve,' said Gwenno.

'Gwenno always wants to reorganise everything,' Elin told Alwena.

'They're supposed to be making it a site of Special Scientific Interest,' said Alwena. 'I think that's what it's called. It's all part of the plan.'

'Be good to explore it, though,' said Gwenno. 'Now then, which way?'

Alwena said, 'Well, if we go up the east drive, it's more wooded. It won't be as cold.' She had managed to look at one of the estate maps while her father had been out of his office for a moment that morning, and had been relieved to see that the Church was on the main road a few yards from the gates of the East Lodge. The drive was rough, but kept clear for occasional farm traffic.

'These are proper woods, aren't they?' said Gwenno as the trees closed round them. 'Oaks and things. Not a bit like forestry. Pity about all the rhododendron. They say it's a weed. Must be nice in spring, though, all purple.'

'*They shut the way through the woods, seventy years ago,*' said Elin in a low, thrilling voice. 'There's a poem that goes like that. My Mum's always saying it.'

How long was the east drive? Alwena tried to remember the map. If it was the same length as the west drive which was the one they normally used, it would take ages to get there at Bedwyr's pace. The girls might want to turn back long before they reached it.

She gathered her courage and said, 'At the end of the drive, there's an old church. There's something inside I need to look at.'

'Oh, right.'

'Sure.'

The girls spoke quite casually. Alwena thought, if T. J. had told them about the church as well as Gareth, they would have remembered, wouldn't they?

And if Gareth had told them he was planning to visit it, they would surely have remembered that too. They'd probably have gone with him, now that Gwenno had a car. So they don't know, she thought, they don't know he might be there.

She hoped he would not be now, because if he was it would look as though the reason she wanted to go there was to see him.

They couldn't really think that, she thought. How would I know he was coming? Besides, if they hadn't offered to take me out on Bedwyr I wouldn't have been able to get near the church. Mum wouldn't have taken me and Dad never would.

By the east gate stood the shell of a lodge cottage similar to T. J.'s and another pair of fallen gate posts.

'I can't see a church,' said Gwenno. 'Oh yes, I can, just up the road. I can see the tower. Oh, I know where we are now. This is the Rhayader road, isn't it?'

'Yes, I think so.'

'Funny shaped tower,' said Elin as they pushed open the iron gate into the churchyard.

'Gothick, c-k,' said Gwenno. 'I bet it was built at the same time as the Plas.'

'It's quite tidy, isn't it?' said Elin. 'Do they still have services here?'

Alwena did not know. She looked at the church's

battlemented tower. Bedwyr snatched at the bit. He pulled the reins out of Alwena's hands and stuck his head down into the grass, tearing it up with his long old teeth and munching it greedily.

There was no sign of Gareth or Llŷr.

'Get the donkey's head up, Elin, he'll get colic if he gorges like that,' said Gwenno. 'Do you want to go inside the church, Alwena? Can you get off, or shall I lift you?'

'I can manage, I think.' She slithered awkwardly to the ground, balancing herself against Bedwyr for a moment, then standing up straight. 'I'll just pop in for a minute.'

'There's no hurry. We'll hold Bedwyr for you.'

T. J. can't have told them about the church, thought Alwena. They'd be making notes about it for their project if he had.

She pulled open the wire mesh gates into the church porch and pushed cautiously at the heavy oak door into the church itself. When it did not open she tried to turn the iron ring of the door latch but could not move it.

Alwena nearly cried out in disappointment. It couldn't be locked, not after she had come all this way.

'Can you manage?' called Gwenno. She came into the church porch, grasped the iron ring firmly and turned it. The latch lifted with a click and the door swung open.

'There you go.'

She peered in over Alwena's shoulder. 'It's nice and plain, isn't it? I like the roof.' She wandered in after Alwena and walked down the aisle towards the altar. Alwena watched her, feeling self-conscious. Now that she was here, she had no idea what she was looking for.

The church seemed quite empty, apart from a few rows of limed oak pews and a dusty stone font which stood to the left of the door. Light filtered in through narrow windows patterned with medallions of stained glass. Alwena ran her fingers over the font's worn surface, tracing the outline of old carvings which had almost worn away with age.

'Hullo,' said Gwenno. 'There are some pictures here.' She was looking into a glass case which stood in the corner opposite the font. 'There was a big fire here in the thirties—did you know that? They've cut out the newspaper reports.'

There didn't seem to be anything about the Jones-Mortimer family, or the Child, not even a memorial plaque on the white distempered wall. Disappointed, Alwena walked down the aisle past the oak pews to the pulpit, and looked into the choir. Nothing there either. Alwena turned away, feeling at a loss. She watched Gwenno stroll outside again and bend over to read a tombstone.

Perhaps it was a tombstone she should be looking for.

Making for the door Alwena passed what she realised was an alcove partitioned off by a carved screen set with small leaded windows. She stopped and looked through the glass. The light was poor but she could see a large monument made of stone—or was it marble? It was worn—or damaged—so badly that she could not tell what it depicted, but Alwena thought she could make out a carved bed with a figure reclining on it, and what might have been two larger figures bending over it. Broken pieces of carved marble were stacked up against the plinth, including a man's head carved all over with tight curls, a macabre sight which made Alwena's stomach jump in revulsion.

Alwena screwed her eyes up to try to read the inscription on the plinth. Her breath misted the glass and she rubbed it clear with her sleeve.

In memory of Ann, the inscription began.

Alwena moved to the next panel and looked through the glass again.

In memory of
Ann
the only daughter of
Edward and Elizabeth Jones-Mortimer
who died in 1811
in her 27th year
after a long illness

This monument is dedicated by her parents.

In her twenty-seventh year.

Alwena leaned against the screen, pressing her forehead onto the glass.

You *see*, said the Child triumphantly. You *see*.

She'd been twenty-seven. When she'd died.

When she was Alwena's age, nearly fifteen, her life had been more than half over.

Twelve more years to go.

Alwena fumbled for one of the oak pews and sat down. She seemed to hear the Child plump herself down next to her. I *told* you, said the Child.

She'd known, really, all along.

This was the secret. This was what her parents were concealing from her.

Her illness was terminal.

That was why the prognosis was always good. Why they never let her see the doctor on her own. That was why her father was so terribly, desperately anxious to protect her from the world. He believed she only had twelve more years to live. He believed that by keeping her safe at Plas Idaleg he could make time stand still. He could stop the years, keep them from rolling onwards towards the time when she, Alwena, would die, as the Child had died.

*　　*　　*

'Sod it,' said Gareth, as he and Llŷr jumped off their bikes at the churchyard gate. 'What the hell are they doing here?'

'I never said anything,' said Llŷr.

T. J. surely wouldn't have told them about the church, thought Gareth.

Elin and Gwenno were sitting on a flat-topped grave, holding Bedwyr the donkey by the reins while he gorged on churchyard grass.

'Well, hello you guys,' said Gwenno. 'Don't look too pleased to see us, will you?'

'What the hell are you doing here?'

'Charming,' said Gwenno. 'As a matter of fact, we were doing a friend a favour.'

'Alwena wanted to visit the church,' said Elin. 'Now we know why.'

'Give me a break,' said Gareth. 'Where is she? Is she in the church?'

'A rendezvous,' said Elin to Gwenno. 'A tryst.'

'Don't be a fool,' said Gareth. 'Would I have brought Llŷr?' He threw his bike on the grass and made for the church. The other three followed on his heels until he turned on them angrily. 'Look, keep out of this. You don't know what it's about. Just stay outside for a minute, okay?'

'All right,' said Gwenno, holding the others back. 'Might there be something wrong?'

'I don't know,' said Gareth, calming down. 'Just give me a minute.'

He watched as Llŷr and the two girls retreated and went to round up the donkey who had spotted his chance to make off across the churchyard to an even greener patch of grass. Then he lifted the latch of the church door and looked inside. Half way down the aisle he saw Alwena sitting in a pew, head bent to her right as though listening to someone sitting next to her.

So what is it, Gareth asked himself, that's going to explain everything? There seemed to be no sign of the statue Llŷr's father had mentioned. He hovered uncertainly at the back of the church, looking at the plain white walls, taking in the font, and the display case with the old press cuttings about the fire. Then, looking across the pews, he saw the screen. He went up to it and looked through the leaded panes at the remains of the memorial, frowning as he tried to read the inscription on the plinth.

Died in her twenty-seventh year.

He stood still for a long while, taking it in. T. J. was right. It did explain everything.

Gareth did not know whether he wanted to murder Alwena's father, or weep for him.

I shouldn't have told Alwena T. J. said to come here, he thought. Not until I'd seen it for myself.

He walked quietly to Alwena's pew and sat down next to her. She looked up, startled, and immediately looked away again. Her face was flushed but she was dry-eyed.

'Just because she died, it doesn't mean you will,' he said eventually.

'I might do,' whispered Alwena. 'Daddy thinks I will.'

'Because of this girl.'

'He would never tell me about her. They would never tell me what happened to her in the end.'

'But it was two hundred years ago. They cure illnesses nowadays.' As he spoke he remembered a cousin of Elin's who had died of leukaemia at the age of twelve. The whole town had gone to her funeral. Gareth remembered his father with tears pouring down his face.

'The prognosis,' said Alwena. Her voice faded, and she gave a little sigh. She began to touch the knuckles of her left hand with the fingers of her right. Her hands were shaking.

She did not weep, but Gareth wanted to. He thought of his father weeping. He thought of Roscoe Morgan. It was as though the man was already mourning his lost daughter. Anger and grief swept over him. He's not giving her a chance, he thought. She might as well be dead already. Yet he was filled with a terrifying pity for the man.

It's Plas Idaleg, he thought. It's as if it owns him. It wants his daughter for a sacrifice. Gareth swallowed. The thought was disgusting, he'd been watching too many horror films.

He touched Alwena on the shoulder, then impulsively put his arm right round her. She caught her breath and looked up at him.

'It's a pity that statue didn't get burned down completely,' he said.

'People would still know,' said Alwena.

'Yes, but they might not remember it so much. They wouldn't lumber *you* with it as though it was your flaming destiny.' Suddenly he was terribly angry. I'd like to kill her father, he thought. Somebody ought to tell him.

'I keep thinking of her,' said Alwena quickly. 'The Child. It's as if she's talking to me.'

'She's probably pleased to see you,' said Gareth. 'On her own all these years.'

'Waiting for me,' whispered Alwena. 'Look, Alwena, we can fly!'

'What?'

'That's what she says. In my dream. And then we start falling, and falling—' Her mouth began to tremble.

'Don't,' said Gareth. 'It's only a dream. Dreams never mean the obvious thing. Anyway lots of people have falling dreams. My mother has them.'

She looked up at him again, frowning uncertainly. Something in her dark eyes undid Gareth. He bent forward and kissed her on the cheek.

Behind them, someone coughed softly.

'Everything all right?' asked Gwenno. She looked carefully at Gareth, and he saw her registering the fact that his cheeks were wet. 'Sorry—shall I go—?'

'No,' said Alwena. 'It's quite all right, Gwenno.' She stood up. 'I'm sorry to keep you waiting.' She rubbed her hands down her parka and said quietly, 'I was just looking at the memorial to Ann Jones-Mortimer.'

'Who?'

The church door was pushed open and Elin and Llŷr came in. They followed Gwenno to the screen and peered over her shoulder as she read the inscription. Gareth fished a dirty handkerchief out of his pocket and blew his nose. Alwena watched him seriously. She touched her flushed cheek quickly with her fingers, then put her hand in her pocket.

'So there is a ghost,' said Elin.

'Dad says it was the doctors killed her,' said Llŷr. 'All that bleeding and stuff they used to go in for.'

'Thanks, Llŷr,' said Gwenno, 'for that timely remark.'

'Oh!' said Elin. 'Did she—did the ghost—was it the same illness—oh, Alwena!'

'It was sort of the same,' said Alwena. She smiled shyly at Elin. 'They didn't have physiotherapists in those days.'

'You've got to ride again,' said Elin. 'You've just got to. I'll help you.'

'I'd like that,' said Alwena.

'We'd better get back,' suggested Gwenno gently. 'Your Mum and Dad will be wondering what's happened to us.'

Gareth heard himself say, 'We'll come with you.'

Alwena turned to him and shook her head. 'Better not, today,' she said. 'Dad wouldn't understand. I need to talk to him first, to explain everything properly.'

'But—'

'If you all come to Plas Idaleg next week,' said Alwena, 'it'll be all right. I'll talk to Dad. Then next Saturday—Gareth, you will explain to them, won't you?'

'Explain?'

'About the garden,' said Alwena. She was smiling. Her voice was vigorous. 'You must tell them about the garden. And I'll tell Dad. Then we can go there.'

'I thought it was a secret,' said Gareth.

'Yes it was,' said Alwena. 'It was. But I'm so tired of secrets. They give me dreams.'

Chapter Fourteen

Gareth and Llŷr watched Alwena ride Bedwyr away down the drive, led by Elin and Gwenno. The resolute set of Alwena's back as she rode away to face her father made Gareth feel ashamed to the bottom of his soul.

The boys pushed their bicycles up the hill away from the church in silence. As they reached the passing space where he had first come across the old iron gate Gareth stopped.

'You carry on home,' he said to Llŷr. 'I'll see you later.'

'Where are you going?'

But he had already dumped his bike in the hedge and was plunging along the overgrown track in the direction of the Plas.

*   *   *

'They seem nice girls,' said Alwena's father.

He seemed to have calmed down a bit since the morning's crisis over the Western Mail article. She gathered that press releases had been faxed and statements made. The whole University had rallied round to support the Plas Idaleg project.

'We'll get there yet,' he'd said, quite jovially, to Elin and Gwenno, as they'd sat in the kitchen drinking coffee after helping Alwena unsaddle Bedwyr and fill up his bucket and haynet.

He'd made himself tea and joined them, chatting about driving tests and donkeys. He had made no comments about them keeping Alwena out too long and tiring her out. He had not even asked where they had taken her, and Elin and Gwenno had honoured Alwena's request not to mention the church.

'See you next week,' they said to Alwena as they departed, and her father had echoed 'See you next week' with her.

They were going to Aberystwyth tonight, with Gareth and Llŷr. To a dance. A foursome. She didn't mind, because Gareth had kissed her. She didn't mind anything now.

'Will Mam be long?' she asked, following her father to the Octagon Library after they had washed up the tea things.

197

'I shouldn't think so. She was going to pick up a prescription for T. J. She's probably dropping it off. She wanted to make sure he was looking after himself properly.'

'Is T. J. ill?'

'His asthma has been quite bad lately. He's getting to be an old man.'

'I hope he's all right,' said Alwena. 'I can't imagine Plas Idaleg without T. J.'

'Neither can I,' said her father with a sigh. He fetched a file out of his office and sat down at the library table with it. He pushed a new ink cartridge into his fountain pen. Alwena moved a chair so that she could sit opposite him. Might as well get it over with.

'This afternoon—' she began.

'Yes,' said her father absently, taking some documents out of the file and glancing at them. 'Did you have a nice ride? Where did you go?'

'We went as far as the church.'

Her father looked up with a frown. 'I don't think they should have taken you on the main road.'

'It was only about ten yards,' said Alwena. 'There was no traffic about.'

'That's not the point—cars come down that hill so fast, you don't see them until they're on top of you. Alwena—'

'I've been into the church, Daddy.'

'What?'

Clasping her hands painfully in her lap, she watched her father. He tried to screw the cap back on his fountain pen, his hands jerking clumsily. Ink splashed onto his notebook.

198

'T. J. told Gareth that if he went to the church he'd find out about the Jones-Mortimers. I wanted to see what he meant.'

Her father dropped the pen, slamming his hand down on it to stop it rolling away.

'*What!*'

'I wanted—'

'So!' said her father furiously, 'Friend Gareth is still on the scene is he, poking his nose into things that don't concern him! And you, Alwena, going behind my back yet again, it seems.'

'I'm not going behind your back,' said Alwena. 'That's why I'm telling you.' She paused, facing him steadfastly. 'I had to know, Daddy. It's my life. I have a right to know.'

'So you don't believe your mother and I know what's best for you any more? That we want to protect you and look after you?'

'I'm not the Child, Daddy,' said Alwena. 'I'm not a bit like the Child. I'm not going to die when I'm twenty-seven just because she did. You think because she had the same illness as me I'm going to die like she did. You think I've only got twelve more years like she had.' She lost the thread of what she wanted to say and broke off, panting a little in agitation.

'I've never heard such a silly story in my life!'

'Why didn't you tell me about her then? Why didn't you ever talk about the Child?'

'Precisely because *we* didn't want *you* to think that you were the same as the Child! Really, Alwena, if these are the wicked stories young Gareth has been telling you

I'm going to have some hard words to say to T. J., even if he is ill.'

'Gareth didn't tell me anything,' cried Alwena. 'He hasn't done anything wrong, not once. He's the kindest, nicest person in the world. He's my friend. He doesn't hide things from me.'

'Alwena,' said her father. 'You're forgetting yourself. You're a sick child. You have a very serious illness. It will be a long time before you're well enough to have the same freedoms as these Sixth Formers, if ever—'

'If ever!' said Alwena. 'So you do think I'm going to die! What's the doctor been telling you that he hasn't been telling me? The prognosis is good, he keeps saying! Is that true or is it a lie? I've got a right to know!'

'Alwena!'

'I'm definitely going to see the doctor on my own next time,' she said. 'I shall make him tell me straight. But it doesn't matter. I know, you see—no, Daddy, listen! He kissed me. That's when I knew I was going to live. Not like the Child. Nobody ever kissed the Child, except her parents I expect—'

'He did what!' roared her father.

'Only on the cheek,' said Alwena. 'But don't you see—she never had young men coming to see her, only old ones.'

'No, I do not see!' shouted her father. 'I've never heard such a load of rubbish! I thought your mother had brought you up to have more in your head than *young men*!'

'I don't mean it like that,' said Alwena, tears of

confusion and weariness coming into her eyes. 'You don't understand, do you? It wasn't just him. It was all of them.'

'They *all* kissed you—'

'No!' wailed Alwena, rubbing frantically at her eyes. 'You're not listening—where's Mam—I want Mam—'

'Never mind your mother! Just for once you'll listen to your father!' He stood up, knocking over his chair. 'What did that boy do to you? I'll kill the little bastard!' Storming round to Alwena's side of the table he seized her by the wrists and shook her hard. Her arms jarred in their sockets causing her to scream in pain and protest.

'Kill me as well then!' she sobbed. 'Kill me now! Why wait twelve years? I might as well be dead now as then!'

Her father released his hold on her wrists, his face aghast. He dropped his forehead onto his fist. Slowly his fingers unclenched and he sat down. 'Alwena,' he said. 'God, Alwena, what's happening? What makes you think I'd ever want you to die?'

'You won't let me do anything,' wept Alwena. 'You won't let me have any friends. I want my friends to come to Plas Idaleg.'

'Alwena—sweetheart—I want you to be happy.'

Alwena buried her head in her arms, crying hysterically. Her father touched her hair. He stood up, then sat down again and put his hand on her shoulder. She heard him draw a deep breath and release it slowly, then blow his nose. He muttered, 'Oh, Christ.' A few moments later he pushed a bundle of tissues into her hand. She took them shakily and wiped her eyes. When she finally had the courage to look up her father was watching her. His face looked as though it had fallen to pieces and been put together again very clumsily.

He said quietly, 'You're right. It was silly of me not to tell you about the Child.'

The sadness in his voice made her weep again for a moment or two. He took the tissues from her and mopped her face. Presently he said, 'I should have known—when you first fell ill. We should have left then. Your mother wanted us to. But I couldn't bear to, you know. There's so much left to do—so much to be put right—Sir Vernon—and I was the last one—and I know T. J. wanted me to see it through—'

'Daddy?'

Her father rubbed his hands over his face. He looked exhausted. At the other end of the building a door opened and closed. 'Thank goodness,' he said. 'That must be your mother.'

His voice trailed off and he stared over Alwena's shoulder.

'Are you all right, Alwena?' asked Gareth.

Alwena caught her breath. Her father started to his feet, then sank back slowly into his chair.

Gareth came into the room. His legs and feet were muddy to the knees. 'I came to see if Alwena was all right,' he said to her father.

'You thought she might not be?'

For a moment Alwena thought her father was going to lose his temper again. He clenched his fists and opened them again. Then he sighed, and said roughly, 'You did right.' The young man and the older one faced each other.

'Sit down, Gareth,' said Roscoe Morgan.

A great weight seemed to fall from Alwena's shoulders. Relief flooded her arteries like a blood transfusion. She reached over and took her father's hand. 'I told him not to come, but I'm glad he did,' she said.

Gareth pushed back his hair self-consciously.

'You're covered in mud,' said Roscoe Morgan. 'Where on earth have you been?'

'I bet I know,' said Alwena. 'Shall I tell him, Gareth, or will you?'

'I don't mind,' said Gareth with his quick smile.

'Tell me what?' asked her father. 'Oh good, I can hear Olwen, your mother must be back.'

'About the garden,' said Alwena. 'The Child's Garden.'

*   *   *

The heather was purple in the Child's Garden; the sky blue, the distances hazy. Alwena and her friend Bethan sat on the rock above the waterfall letting the cold water of the stream run over their feet. Nearby Elin and Gwenno had thrown a blanket over a patch of turf, and stripped down to their bikinis to sunbathe. Gareth lay on his front in the heather reading the latest Terry Pratchett and Llŷr could be heard trampling through the trees searching for fungi, using Olwen as a truffle hound.

It was the last weekend of the summer holidays.

'Look at him,' said Elin to Gwenno, jerking her head at Gareth. 'We don't see him all summer, and when we do, blow me, he brings a book and we don't get a peep out of him.'

'It'll be my last light reading until next July,' said Gareth, not looking up.

He had spent the whole summer working in the office of Bennett Evans Associates. Architecture was no longer something he dreamed about; it was something he did, like Gwenno and her music. Even his father took it for granted.

He rested his chin on his arms, looking across at Alwena and drowsily remembering the past year. She was taller, browner and livelier than when he had first met her last autumn. They were still close, but she no longer blushed when he smiled at her. She had many other friends, and two years was suddenly a big age gap. It was the gap between people doing their GCSEs and people doing their A Levels. This year, this crucial year, he needed to be with his contemporaries: Elin, Gwenno and Llŷr.

He got on pretty well with Elin these days. They knew where they stood with each other.

'The summer's over before it's even started. We never even looked for those pets' gravestones you said about,' said Bethan to Alwena. 'Now it's back to boring old school. Boring old GCSEs, why were they ever invented?'

'Boring,' echoed Alwena. She did not really mean it. Since starting school at Abercoed in January she had not had a single minute to spare for being bored. Also, a most important thing had happened. Her class had been taken to Stratford-upon-Avon where she had seen a play performed for the first time in her life, in a real theatre with professional actors. It had transformed everything.

From that moment she knew with perfect clarity that her whole life would be about making plays. You could put everything into plays, everything you lived and saw and feared and dreamed. You could put the Child into a play, or T. J. or Sir Vernon Roderick or Llŷr's Nain, and they would all be just as real or as fantastic as each other, as you chose.

'How's T. J., Alwena?' asked Gareth, picking up her train of thought as he could still do in an uncanny way.

'Better, I think,' she replied. 'We don't see so much of him these days, though.' She was not sorry about this. She loved T. J. but he carried too much history about with him, waiting to load it on you. He'd loaded her father with more than he could carry, and it had nearly destroyed him. She smiled across at Gareth, knowing that this was an understanding they would always share.

The midges were swarming as they picked up the remains of their picnic and loaded it onto Bedwyr who had been endowed with a new career as pack-donkey since the path up to the garden had been restored. This job had been carried out in the Spring under the foremanship of Bryn Lloyd.

Gareth had known that once the project had been started his father would not be able to keep his nose out, and so it had proved.

Before they left, Gareth climbed up the rocks to the highest viewpoint, lifting Alwena up in front of him.

'Can you still see cities out there?' she asked as they looked out over the mountains.

'Oh yes—London, Bristol, Manchester—'

'Oh dear, not Venice and Vladivostock?'

'Next year.'

They laughed.

'You're not frightened of falling off any more, then,' said Gareth.

'No,' said Alwena. 'I'm getting better at hanging on to the rock face.' She made clawing gestures at Gareth. Her hands were still bent, but she had developed an expressive way of using them.

'Look at the way the light changes when that big cloud crosses the sun,' she said. 'It's pure theatre.'

She could never keep off her new passion for very long.

'Do you ever think about the Child?'

'Oh yes, all the time,' said Alwena. 'But she's all right, you know. Do you remember that dream I had that I told you about?'

'Oh yes, the falling dream.'

'Not falling,' said Alwena. 'Flying.'

Author's Note

This story was inspired by the short life of Mariamne Johnes (1784-1811), daughter of Thomas Johnes of Hafod Uchtryd in Ceredigion.

The story of Hafod and the fabulous house and gardens created by Thomas Johnes in the mountains beyond Devil's Bridge was made famous by Elisabeth Inglis-Jones's book *Peacocks in Paradise*. The great mansion was demolished in the nineteen fifties and the land taken over by the Forestry Commission, but in more recent years a number of projects have been initiated with the purpose of restoring the old walks and gardens.

For the purposes of my story I have renamed the mansion and resurrected it as it may have looked in Victorian times, but I have taken as many other liberties with the history and geography of the estate and its surroundings as seemed necessary.

A Writer's Bursary awarded by the Literature Panel of the Arts Council of Wales made the completion of this book possible, and is gratefully acknowledged.

Also by Mary Oldham :

SOMETHING'S BURNING

Something's burning in the hearts of four young people in a Welsh border town.

Barbara Dawes burns to be Welsh, to be thin, to have a boyfriend. She's in love with Lord Byron the poet and, more painfully, with Byron Tudor in her class at school.

And Byron Tudor wouldn't mind being adored by her either, if only she weren't what he calls a 'White Settler' from England. He burns to do something for Wales, though what exactly he doesn't know.

Hywel Tudor is Byron's elder brother, a farmer and horse-breeder. Barbara may think he's too old and pushy , but even he is someone whose feelings can be hurt.

Who knows what fire is eating up the heart of Heledd Aeronwy Jones, the mysterious new girl from North Wales who refuses to speak to anyone? Why did she scratch 'I am a political prisoner' on a toilet wall? Who has imprisoned her? Heledd's dumb and desperate anger draws each one of them, like moths to a flame.

PONT YOUNG ADULT
For readers of 13 and over.
£4.95